Hidenori Kusaka

I've finally completed my Gigantamax collection!
I did it all by myself, so it took a while. It was
just one battle after another, but now I have a
real sense of accomplishment. How are your
collections going?

Satoshi Yamamoto

What I like best about *Pokémon: Sword & Shield*:
④ Piers.

D0088684

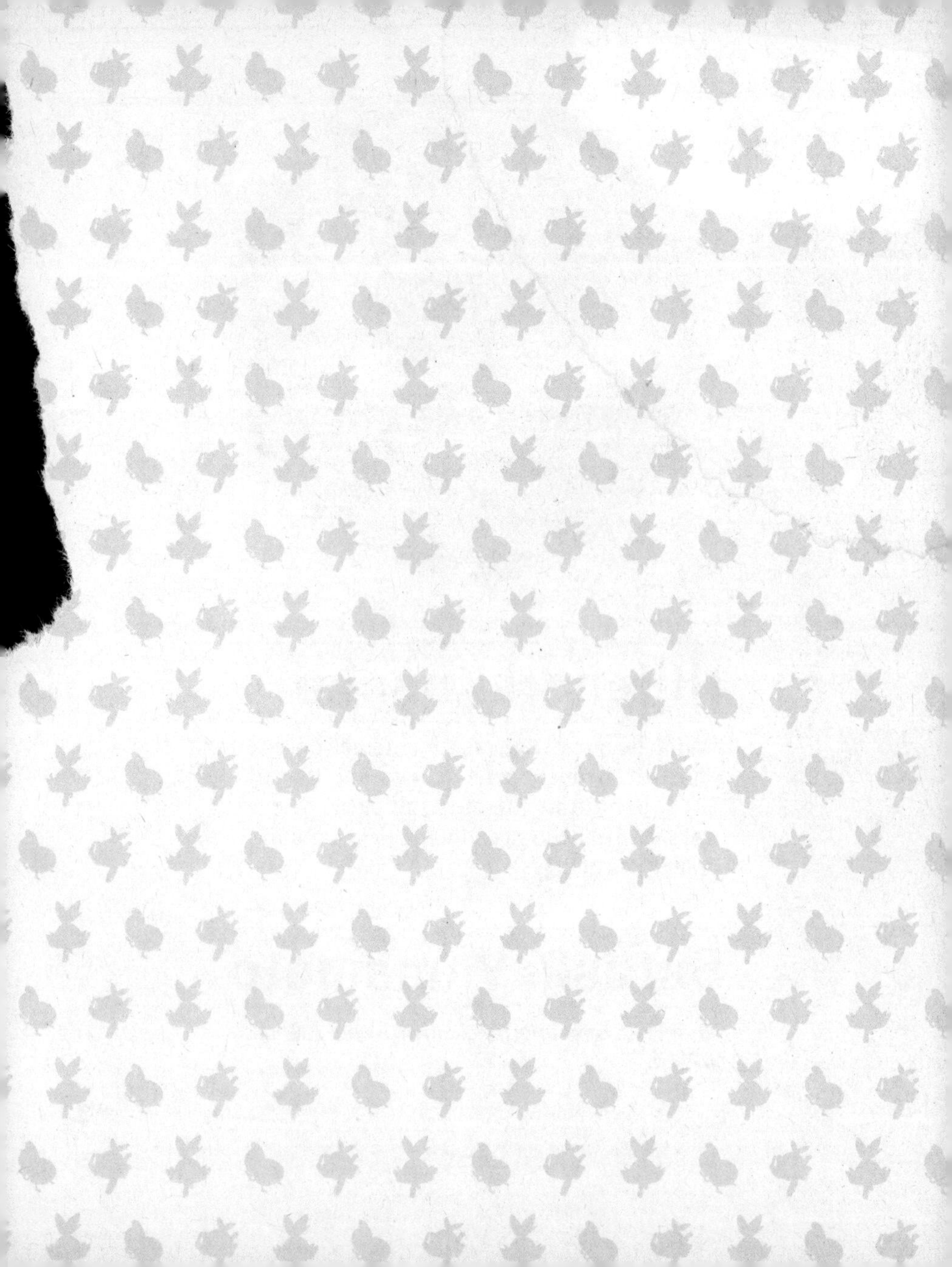

Pokémon

SWORD & SHIELD

7

STORY
Hidenori Kusaka

ART
Satoshi Yamamoto

Henry
SWORD

THE DESCENDANT OF A RENOWNED SWORDSMITH, HENRY IS AN ARTISAN WHO FIXES AND IMPROVES POKÉMON GEAR.

Casey
SHIELD

AN ELITE HACKER AND COMPUTER TECH WHO CAN ACCESS ANY DATA SHE WANTS. SHE'S PROFESSOR MAGNOLIA'S ASSISTANT AND TEAM ANALYST.

The Story So Far

UPON ARRIVING IN THE GALAR REGION, MARVIN SEES A DYNAMAXED POKÉMON AND FALLS OFF A CLIFF! HE IS SAVED BY HENRY SWORD AND CASEY SHIELD AND JOINS THEM ON THEIR JOURNEY TO COMPLETE THEIR GYM CHALLENGE AND DISCOVER THE SECRET OF DYNAMAXING WITH PROFESSOR MAGNOLIA. HENRY CONTINUES TO WIN HIS GYM CHALLENGES, AND CASEY HAS FOUND SOME OF HER POKÉMON. BUT WHAT IS THE MEANING BEHIND THE STRANGE INCIDENTS THAT APPEAR TO FORE-SHADOW AN OMINOUS FUTURE FOR THE GALAR REGION? AND WHAT IS THE MYSTERIOUS LIFE-FORM LURKING UNDERGROUND AT THE ENERGY PLANT?

Marvin

A ROOKIE TRAINER WHO RECENTLY MOVED TO GALAR. HE'S EXCITED TO LEARN EVERYTHING HE CAN ABOUT POKÉMON!

Professor Magnolia

A FAMED RESEARCHER WHO STUDIES DYNAMAXING, THE GIGANTIFICATION OF POKÉMON. SHE IS A GENTLE SOUL WHO IS FOND OF DRINKING TEA.

Leon

LEON IS THE BEST TRAINER IN GALAR. HE'S THE UNDEFEATED CHAMPION!

Sonia

PROFESSOR MAGNOLIA'S GRAND-DAUGHTER AND LEON'S CHILDHOOD FRIEND. SHE'S HELPING THE PROFESSOR INVESTIGATE THE GALAR REGION!

CONTENTS

Adventure 20 Cracking!! Brilliant Tap-Dancing

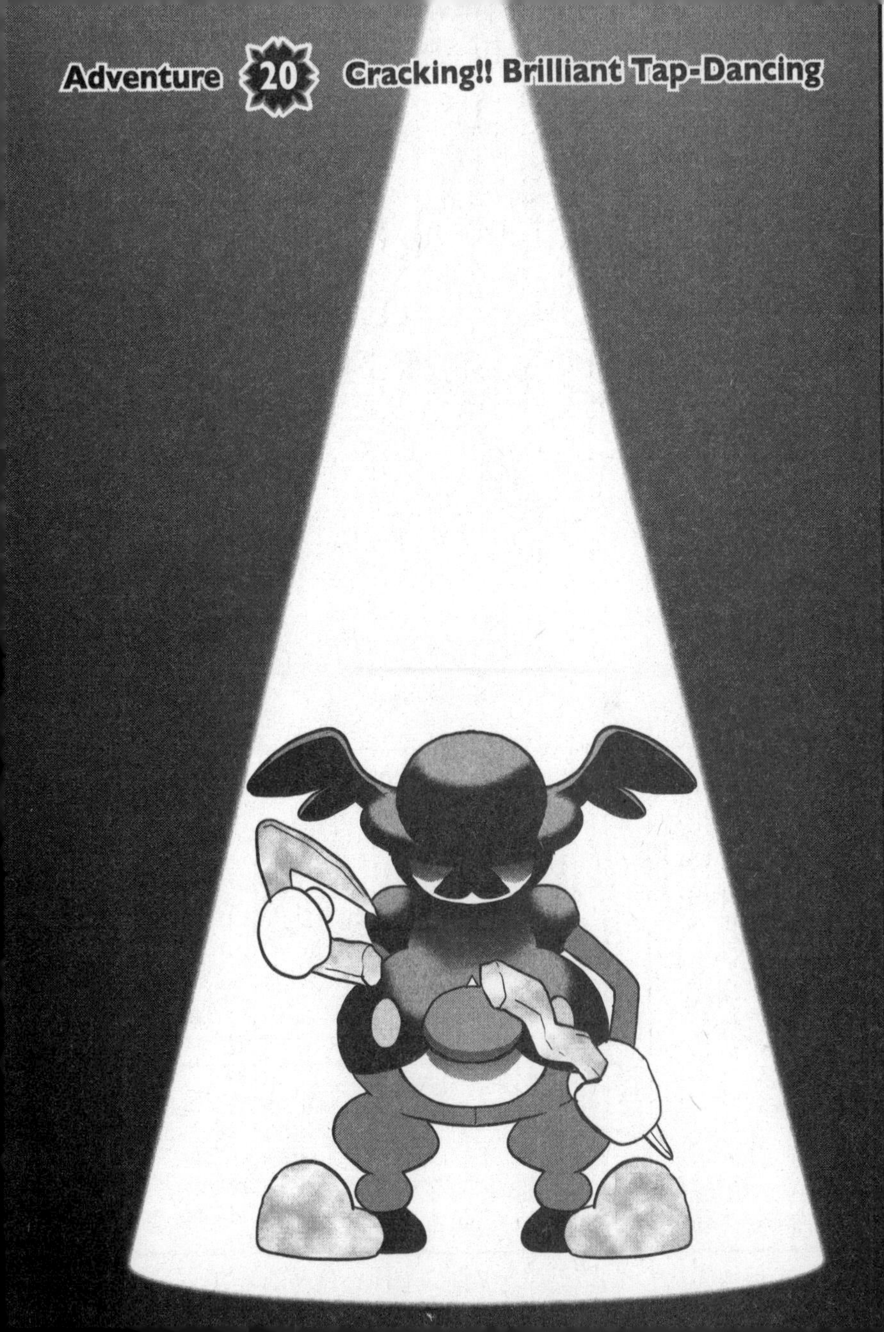

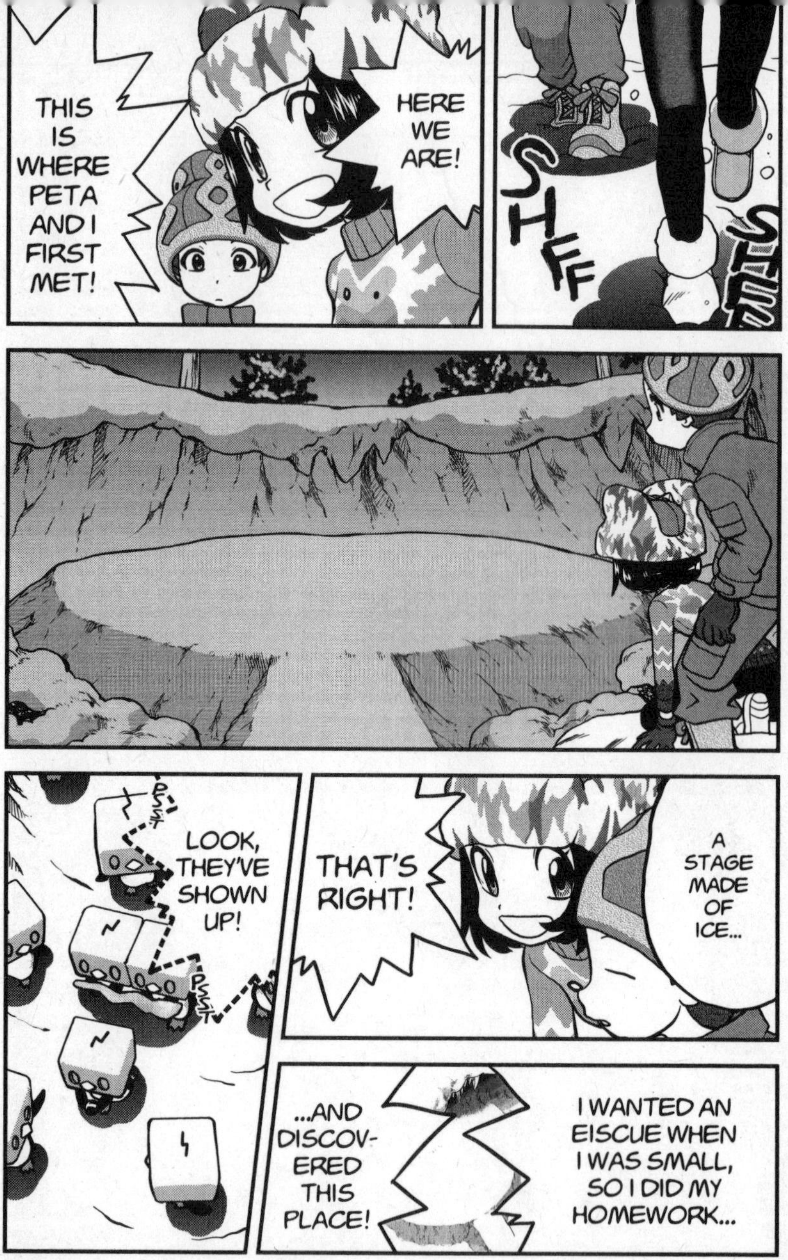
SHFF
HERE WE ARE!
THIS IS WHERE PETA AND I FIRST MET!
A STAGE MADE OF ICE...
THAT'S RIGHT!
I WANTED AN EISCUE WHEN I WAS SMALL, SO I DID MY HOMEWORK...
...AND DISCOVERED THIS PLACE!
PSST
LOOK, THEY'VE SHOWN UP!
PSST

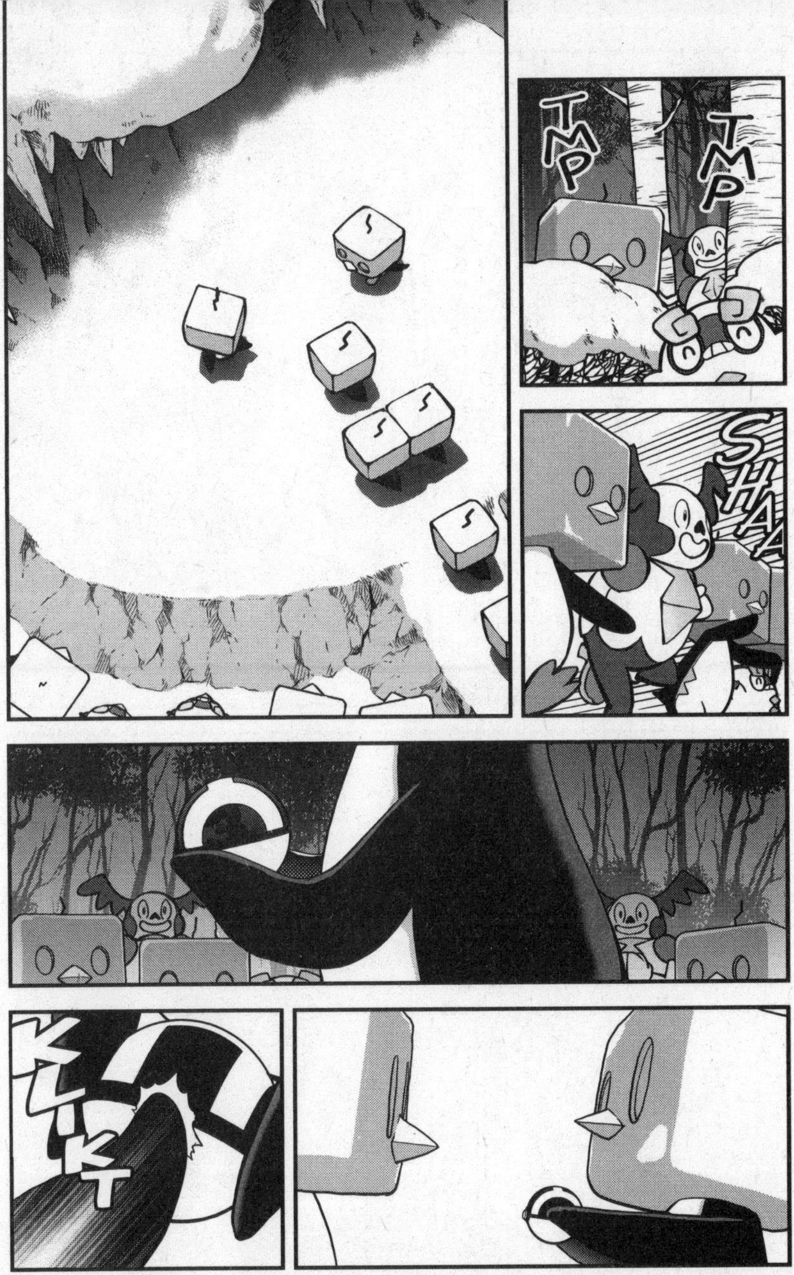
TMP
TMP
SHAA
KLIKT

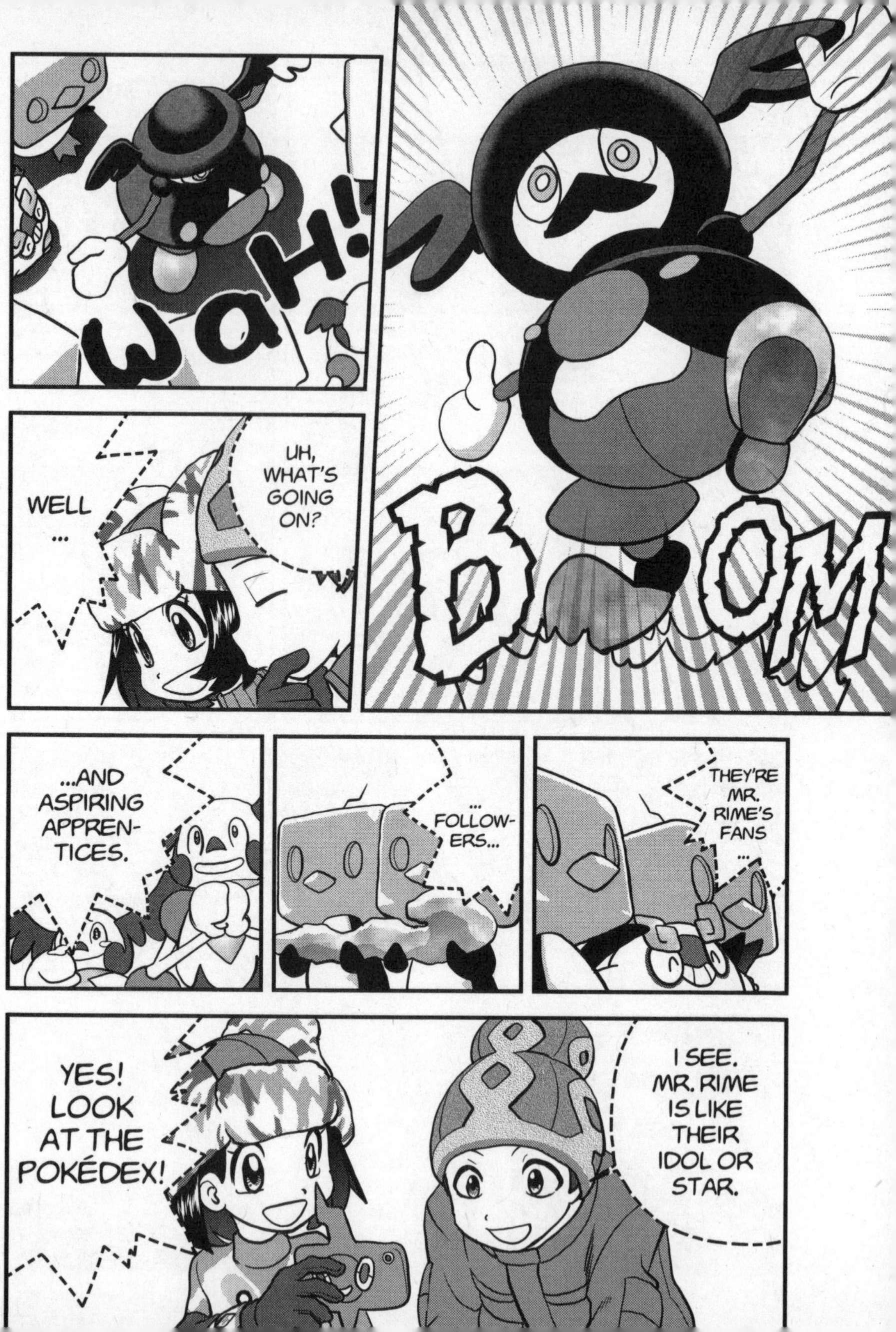
B OM
WAH!!
UH, WHAT'S GOING ON?
WELL ...
THEY'RE MR. RIME'S FANS ...
... FOLLOW-ERS...
...AND ASPIRING APPREN-TICES.
I SEE. MR. RIME IS LIKE THEIR IDOL OR STAR.
YES! LOOK AT THE POKÉDEX!

THAT'S RIGHT!

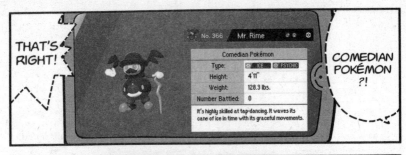

No. 366 — Mr. Rime

Comedian Pokémon

Type:	ICE	PSYCHIC
Height:	4'11"	
Weight:	128.3 lbs.	
Number Battled:	0	

It's highly skilled at tap-dancing. It waves its cane of ice in time with its graceful movements.

COMEDIAN POKÉMON ?!

MELONY'S MR. RIME, WITH THE BROKEN CANE, REALLY IS A STAR!

THAT STAGE IS WHERE MR. RIME PERFORMS ITS TAP DANCE AND COMEDY SHOWS!

THAT'S WHEN I BECAME FRIENDS WITH PETA.

...AND I WAS SO ENGROSSED IN ITS INCREDIBLE TAP DANCE STEPS...

I SAW ITS SHOW...

THE POKÉMON IN THE AUDIENCE HELPED ME, THOUGH.

...THAT I ALMOST FROZE TO DEATH!

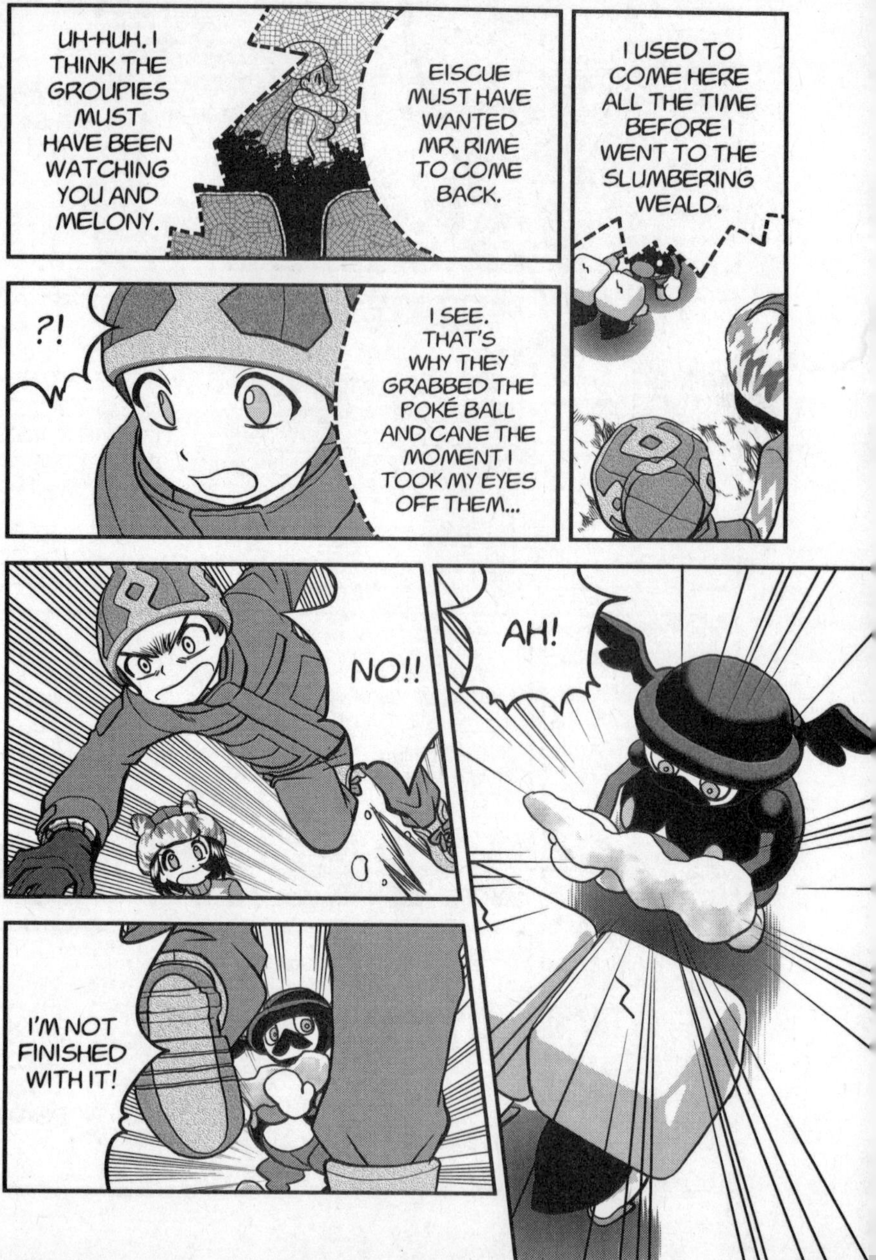
I USED TO COME HERE ALL THE TIME BEFORE I WENT TO THE SLUMBERING WEALD.
EISCUE MUST HAVE WANTED MR. RIME TO COME BACK.
UH-HUH. I THINK THE GROUPIES MUST HAVE BEEN WATCHING YOU AND MELONY.
I SEE. THAT'S WHY THEY GRABBED THE POKÉ BALL AND CANE THE MOMENT I TOOK MY EYES OFF THEM...
?!
AH!
NO!!
I'M NOT FINISHED WITH IT!

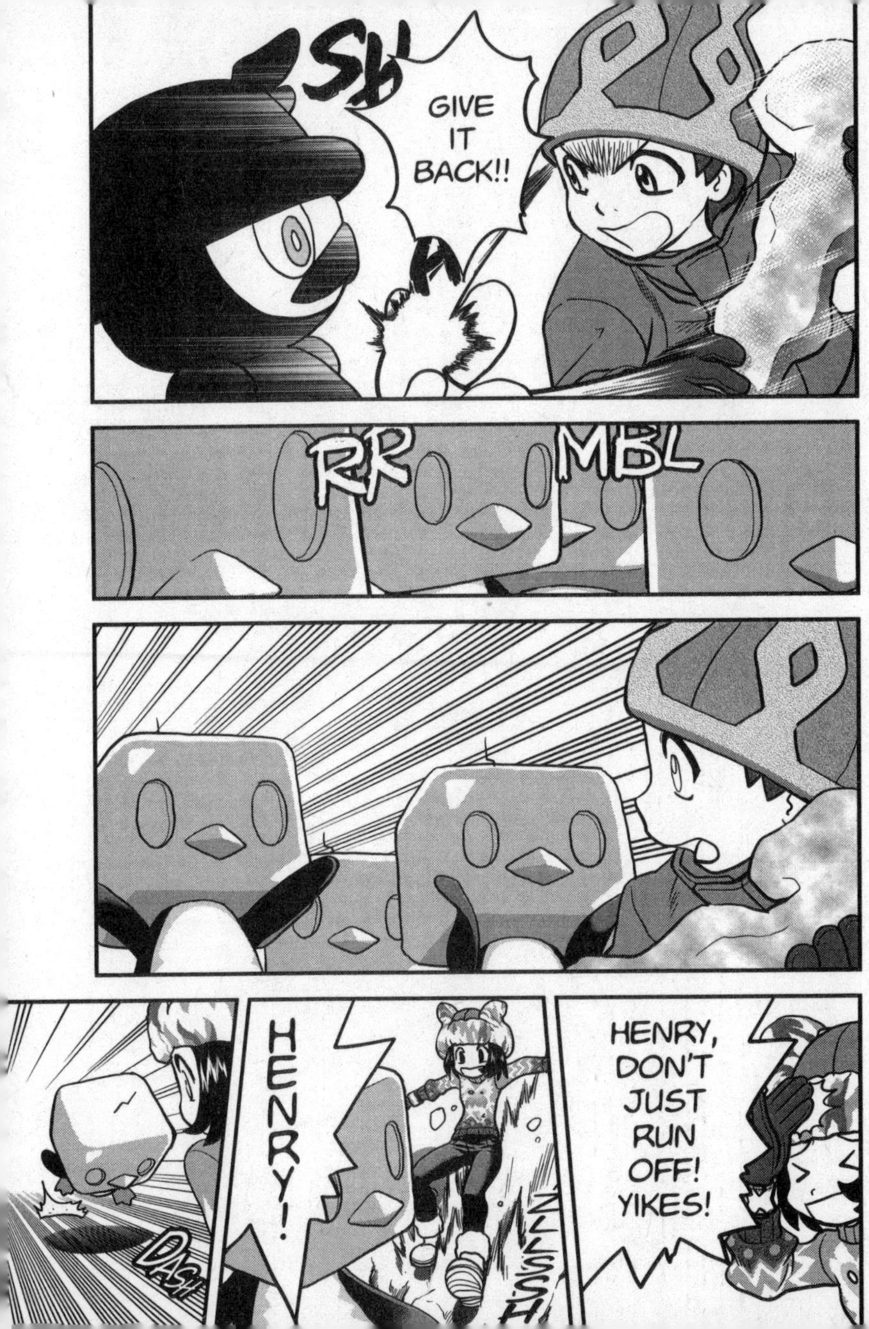
GIVE IT BACK!!
Sh!
RR MBL
HENRY, DON'T JUST RUN OFF! YIKES!
HENRY!
ZLLSSH
DASH

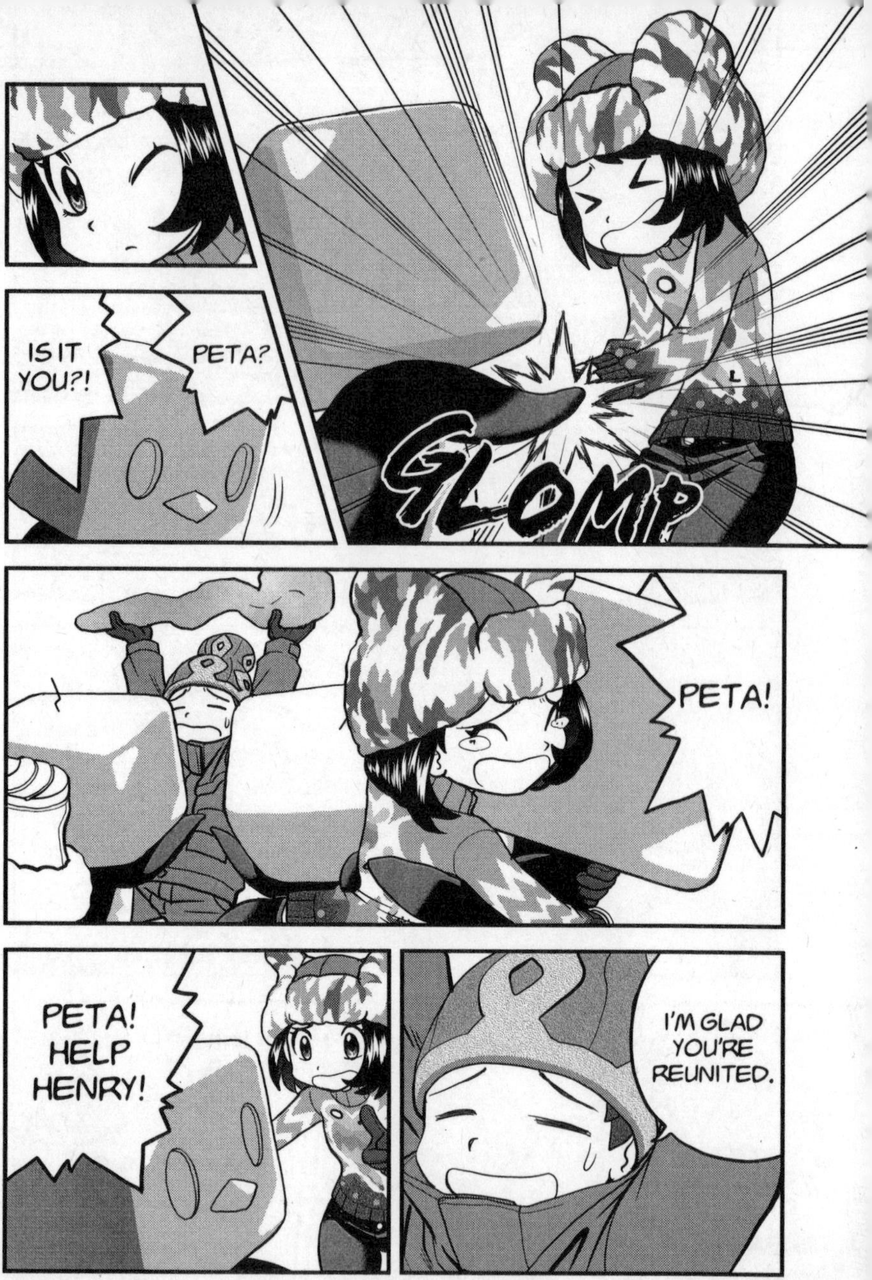
GLOMP
PETA?
IS IT YOU?!
PETA!
I'M GLAD YOU'RE REUNITED.
PETA! HELP HENRY!

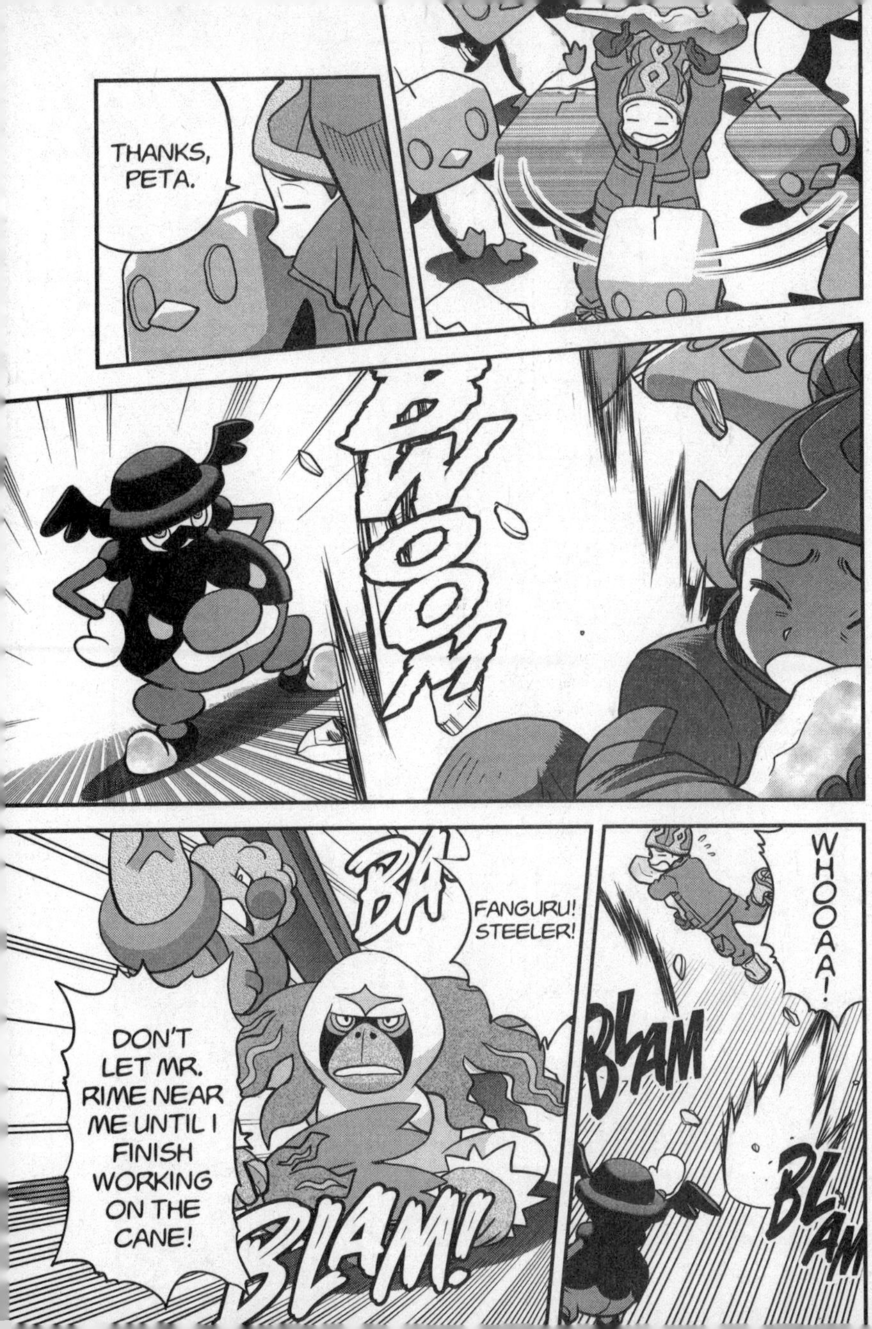
THANKS, PETA.
BVOOOM
WHOOAA!
FANGURU! STEELER!
BA
DON'T LET MR. RIME NEAR ME UNTIL I FINISH WORKING ON THE CANE!
BLAM
BLAM
BLAM!
BLAM

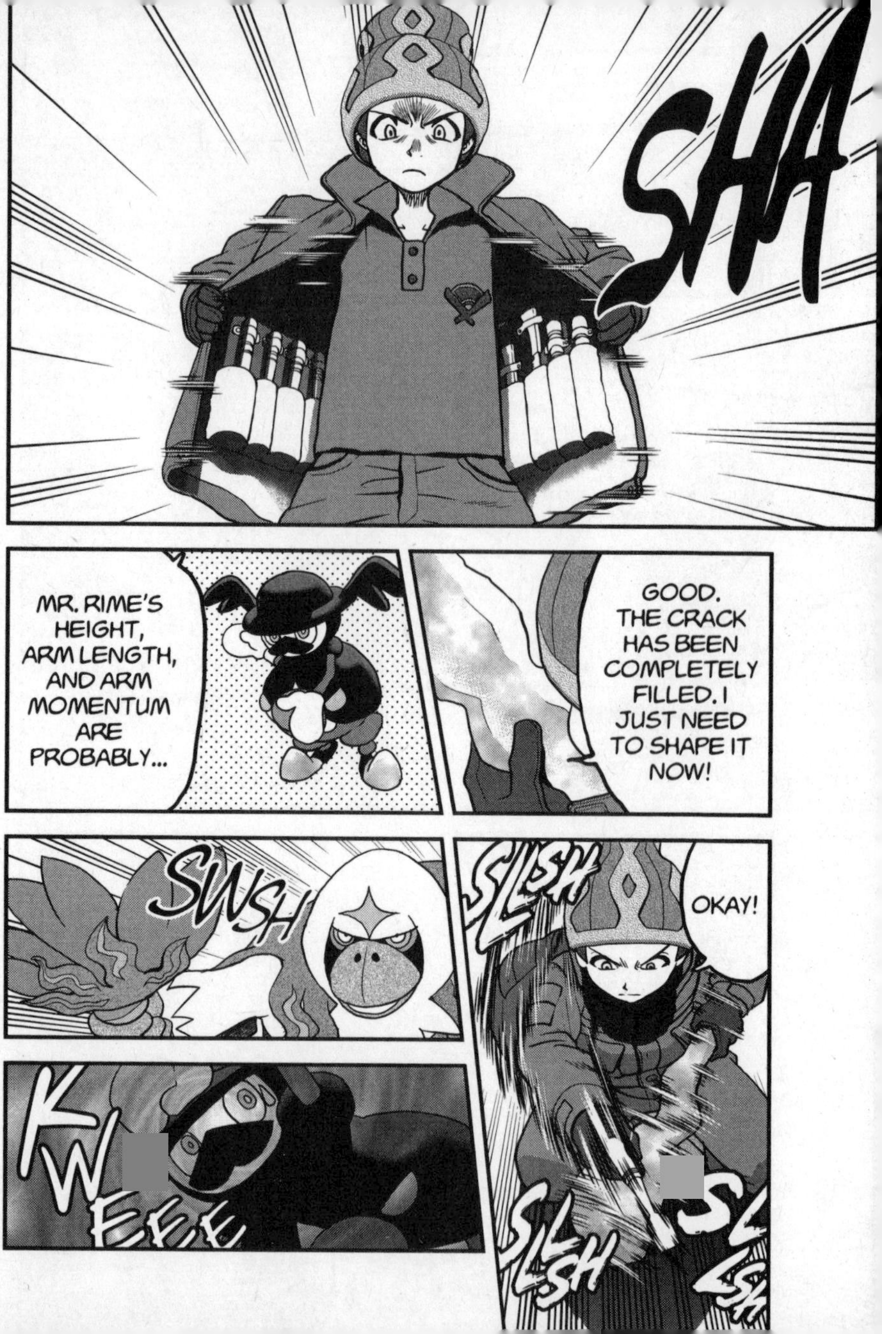
SHA
GOOD. THE CRACK HAS BEEN COMPLETELY FILLED. I JUST NEED TO SHAPE IT NOW!
MR. RIME'S HEIGHT, ARM LENGTH, AND ARM MOMENTUM ARE PROBABLY...
SLISH
OKAY!
SLISH
SLISH
SWSH
KW
EEE

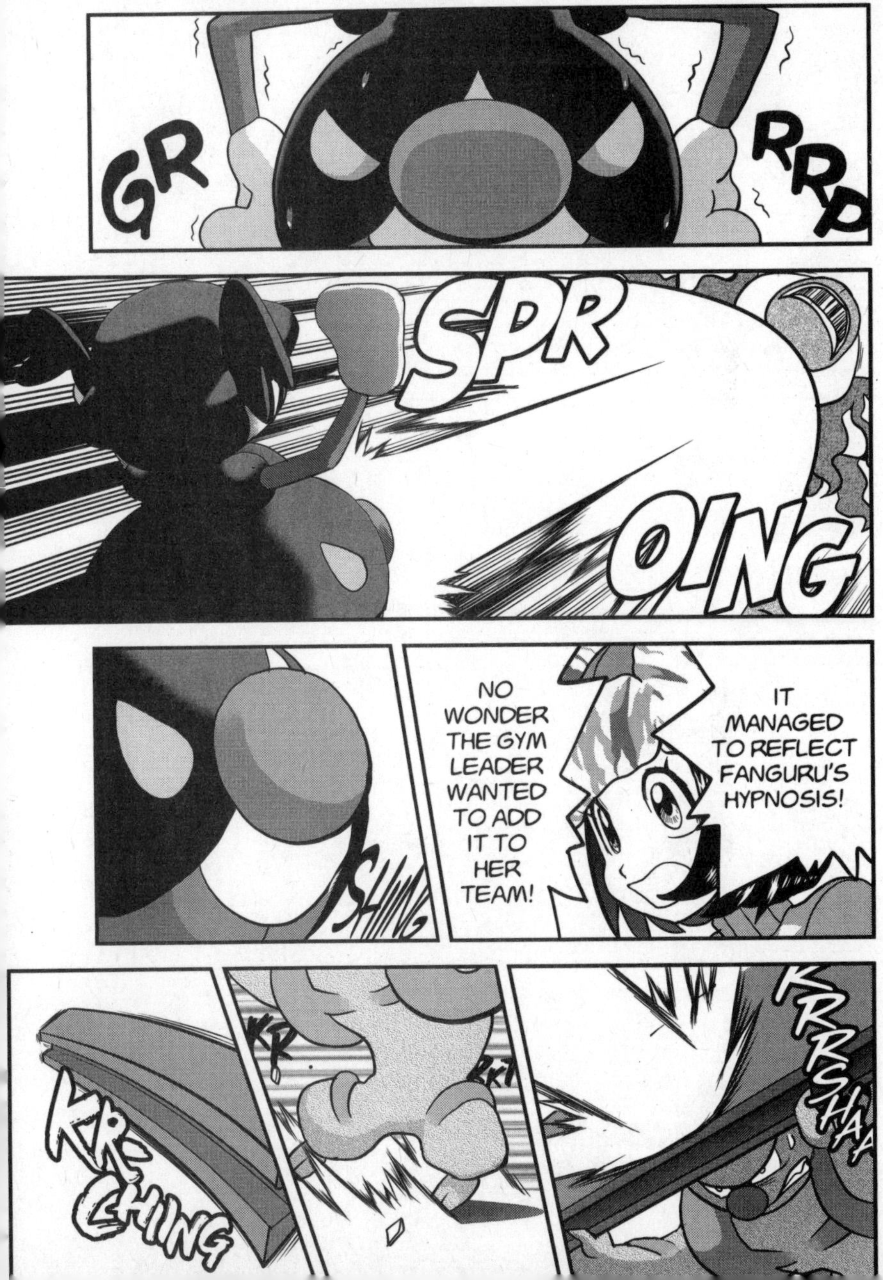
GR
RRRP
SPR
OING
IT MANAGED TO REFLECT FANGURU'S HYPNOSIS!
NO WONDER THE GYM LEADER WANTED TO ADD IT TO HER TEAM!
SHING
KRRSHA
KR
RKT
KR-CHING

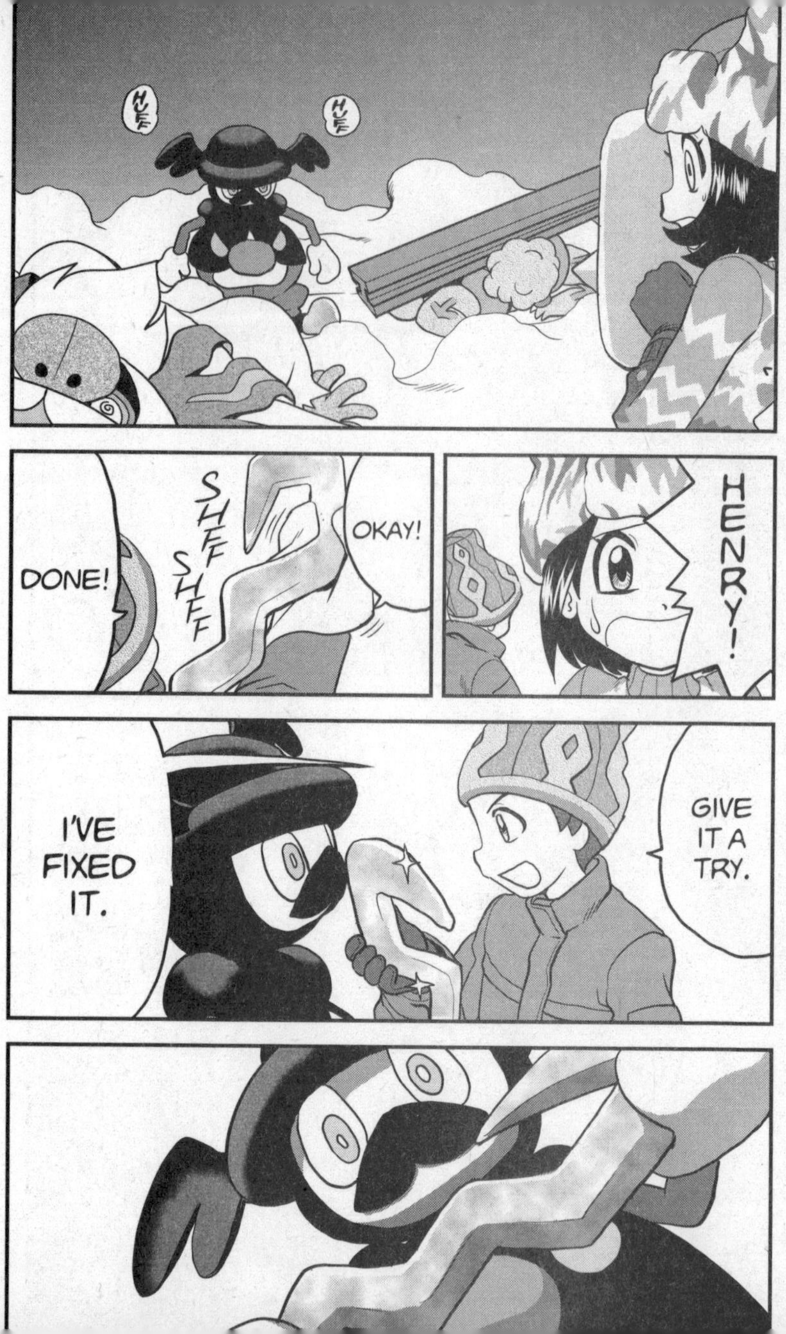
HUFF
HUFF
HENRY!
OKAY!
SHEFF SHEFF
DONE!
GIVE IT A TRY.
I'VE FIXED IT.

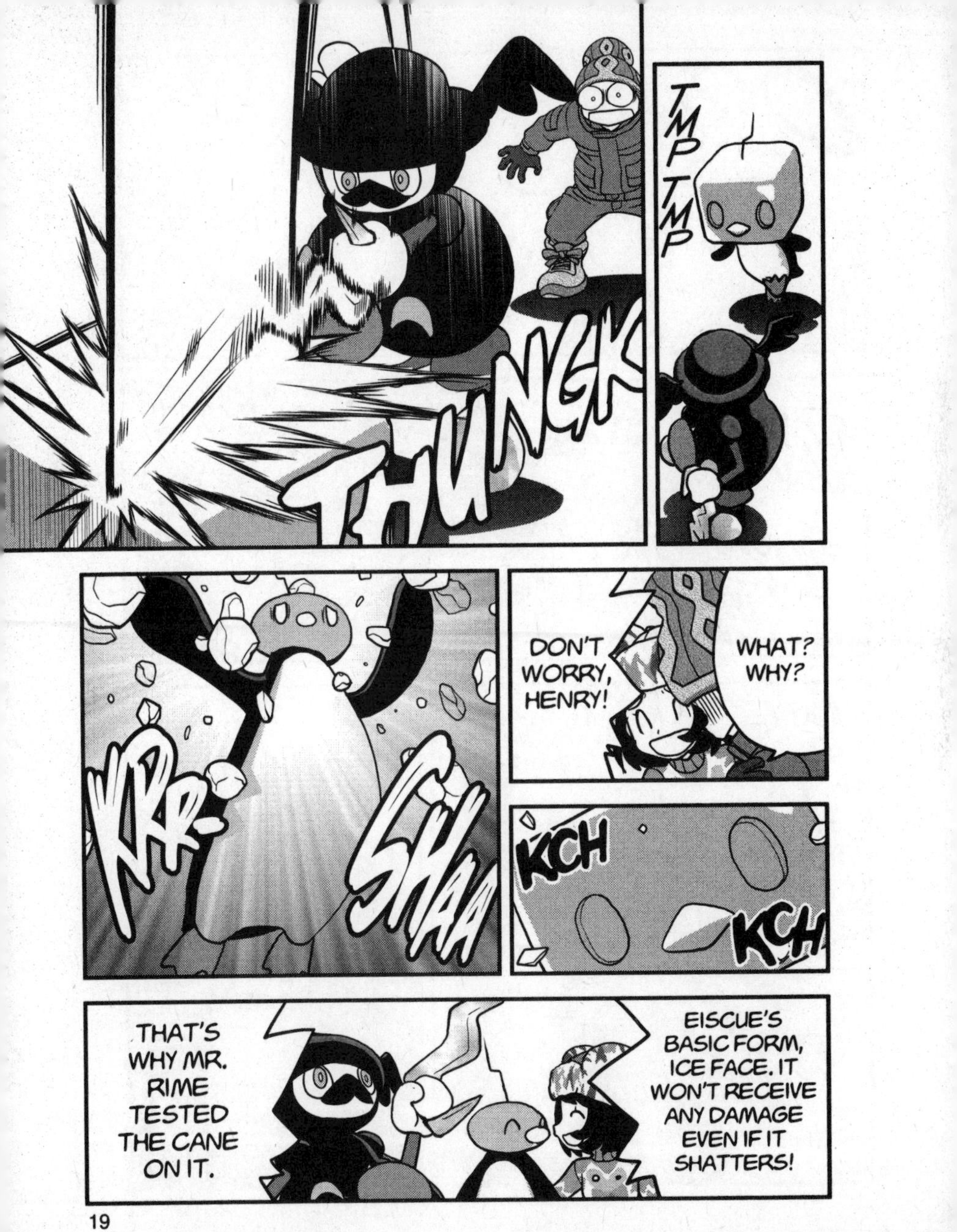
TMP TMP TMP
THUNGK
WHAT? WHY?
DON'T WORRY, HENRY!
KCH
KCH
KRR
SHAA
EISCUE'S BASIC FORM, ICE FACE. IT WON'T RECEIVE ANY DAMAGE EVEN IF IT SHATTERS!
THAT'S WHY MR. RIME TESTED THE CANE ON IT.

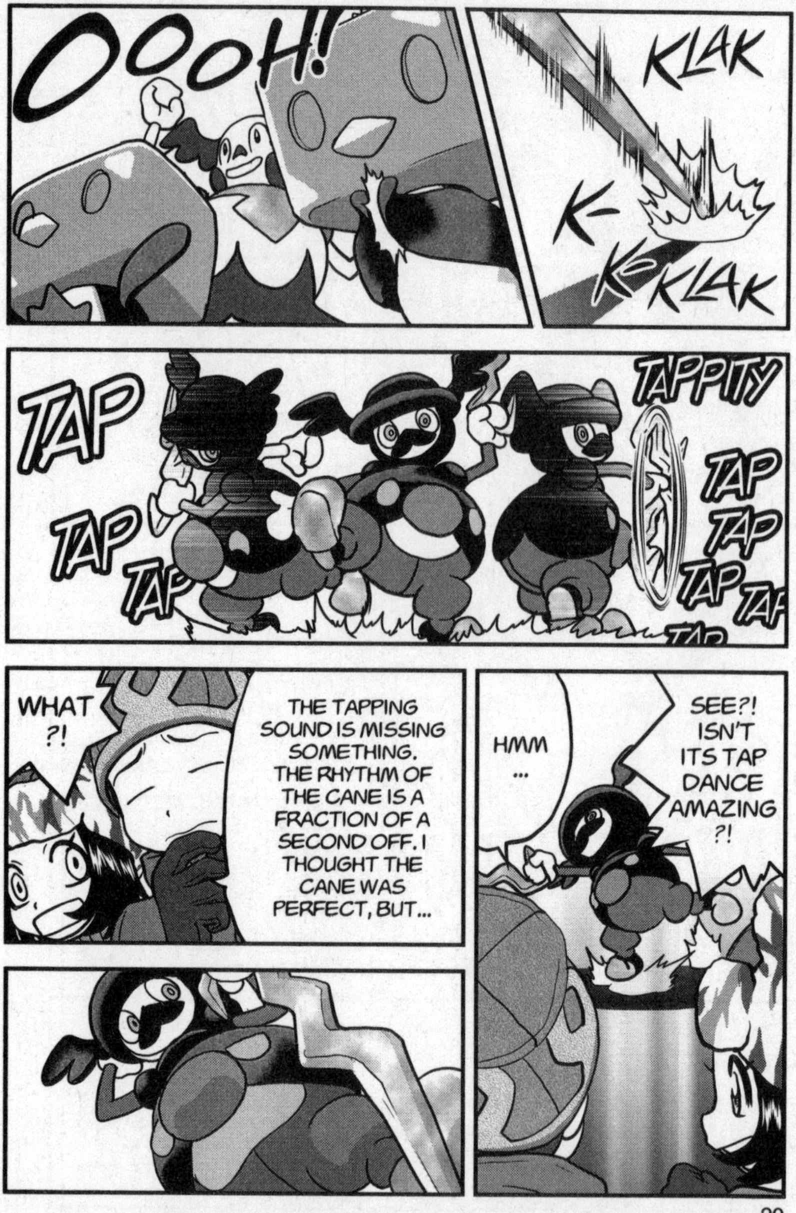
KLAK
K-
K-KLAK
OOOH!
TAPPITY
TAP
TAP
TAP
TAP
TAP
TAP
TAP
SEE?! ISN'T ITS TAP DANCE AMAZING ?!
HMM ...
THE TAPPING SOUND IS MISSING SOMETHING. THE RHYTHM OF THE CANE IS A FRACTION OF A SECOND OFF. I THOUGHT THE CANE WAS PERFECT, BUT...
WHAT ?!

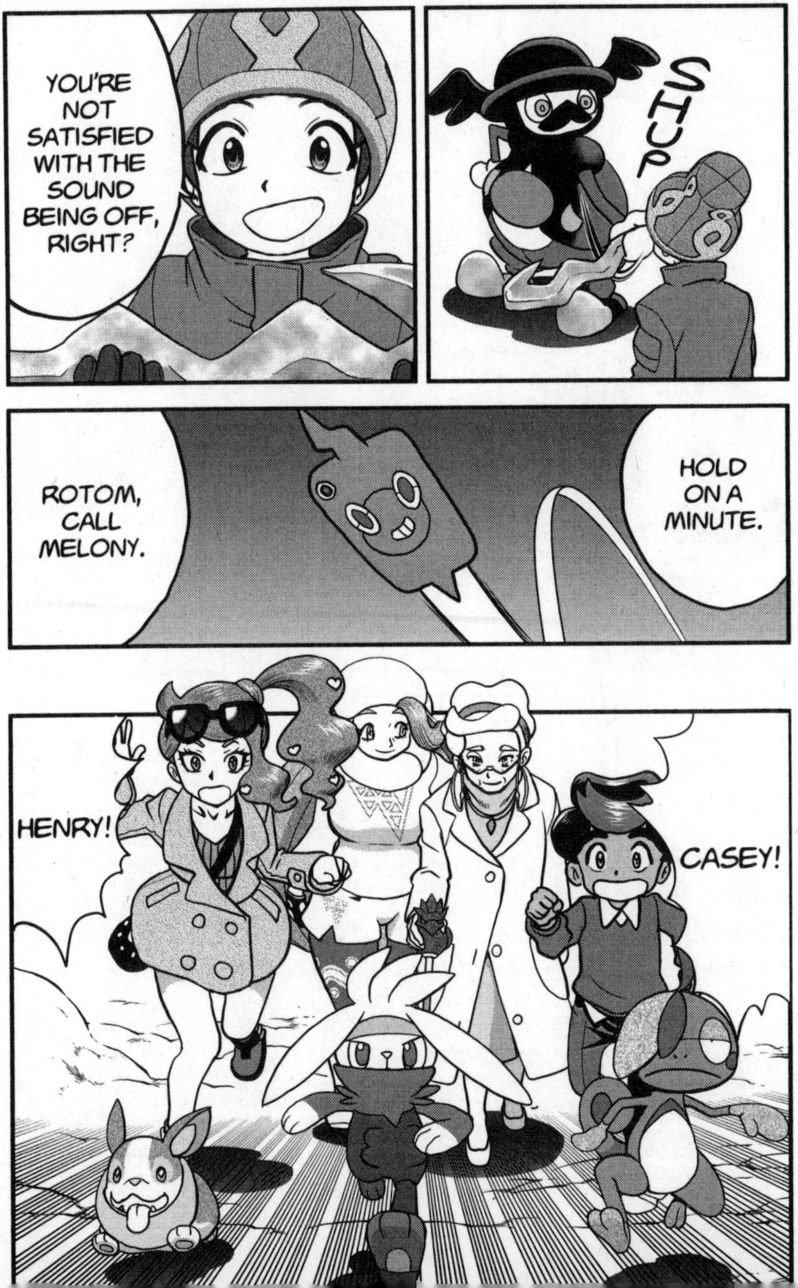
SHUP
YOU'RE NOT SATISFIED WITH THE SOUND BEING OFF, RIGHT?
HOLD ON A MINUTE.
ROTOM, CALL MELONY.
CASEY!
HENRY!

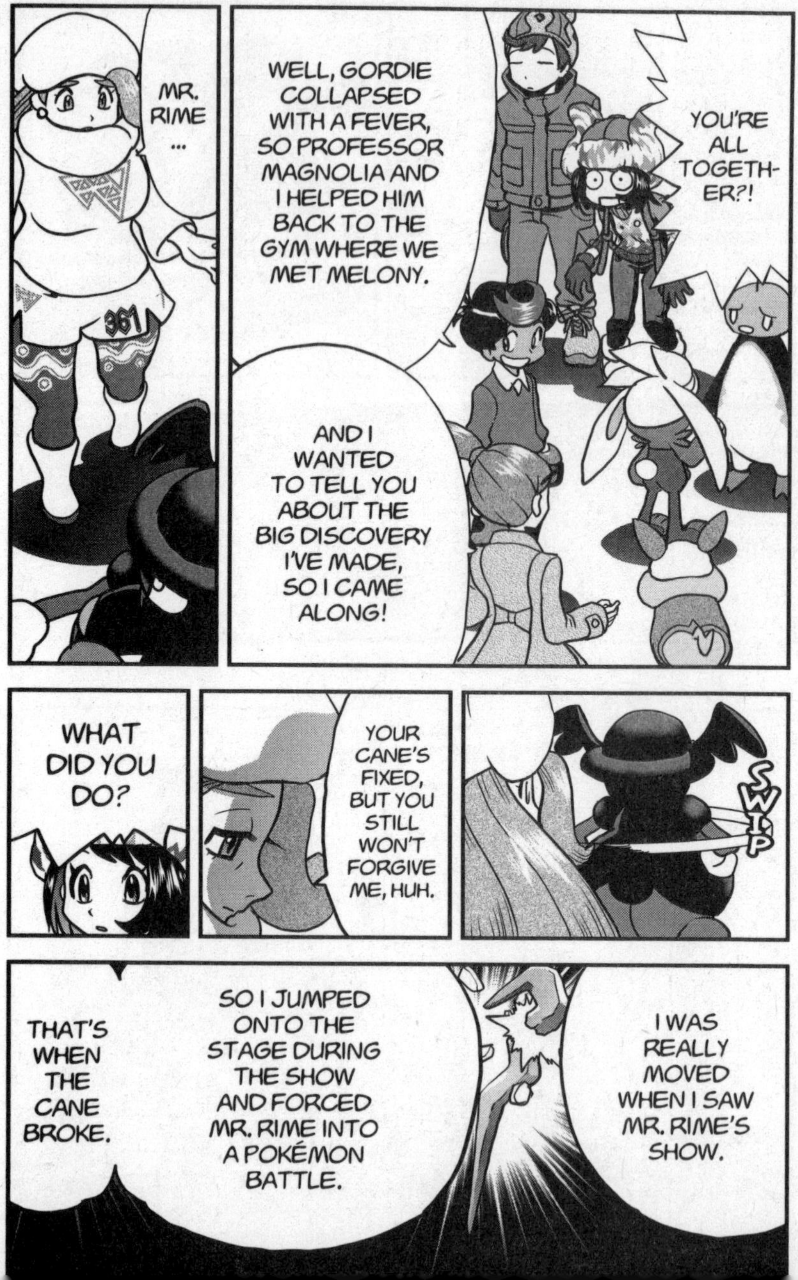
YOU'RE ALL TOGETH-ER?!
WELL, GORDIE COLLAPSED WITH A FEVER, SO PROFESSOR MAGNOLIA AND I HELPED HIM BACK TO THE GYM WHERE WE MET MELONY.
AND I WANTED TO TELL YOU ABOUT THE BIG DISCOVERY I'VE MADE, SO I CAME ALONG!
MR. RIME ...
361
SWIP
YOUR CANE'S FIXED, BUT YOU STILL WON'T FORGIVE ME, HUH.
WHAT DID YOU DO?
I WAS REALLY MOVED WHEN I SAW MR. RIME'S SHOW.
SO I JUMPED ONTO THE STAGE DURING THE SHOW AND FORCED MR. RIME INTO A POKÉMON BATTLE.
THAT'S WHEN THE CANE BROKE.

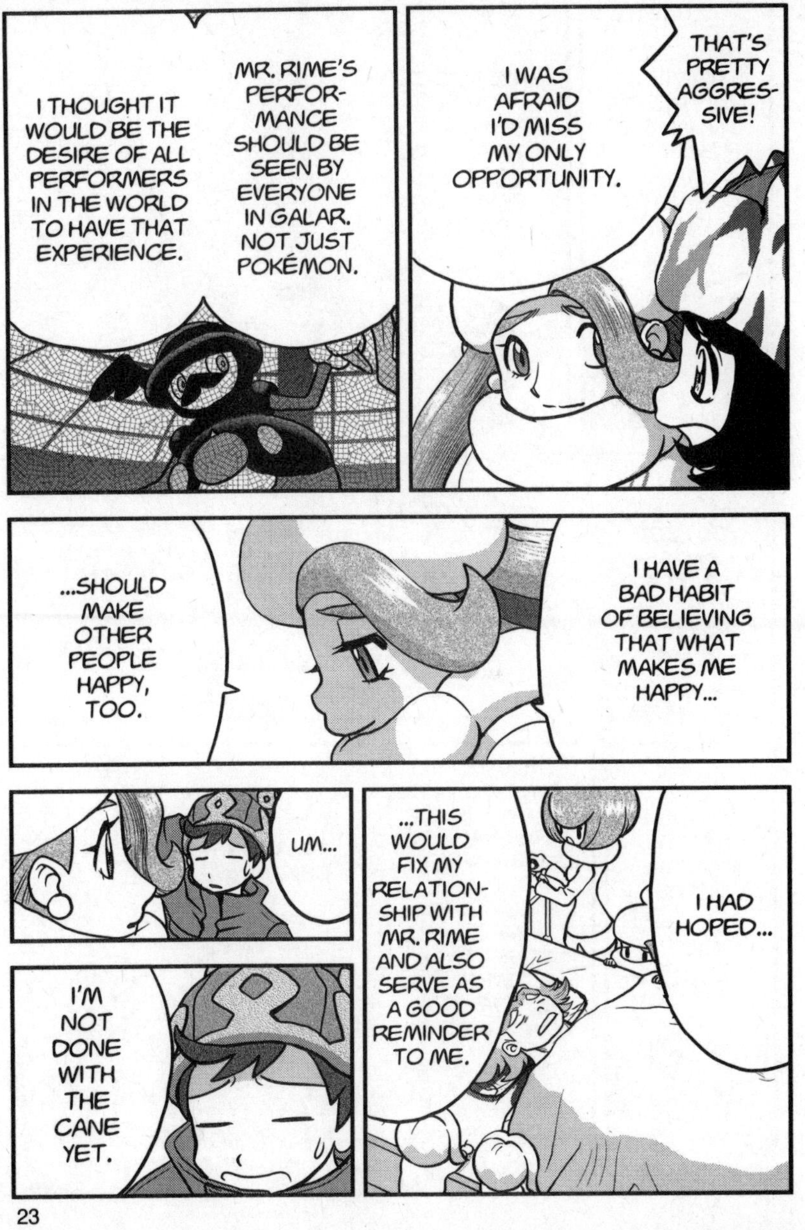
THAT'S PRETTY AGGRES-SIVE!
I WAS AFRAID I'D MISS MY ONLY OPPORTUNITY.
MR. RIME'S PERFOR-MANCE SHOULD BE SEEN BY EVERYONE IN GALAR. NOT JUST POKÉMON.
I THOUGHT IT WOULD BE THE DESIRE OF ALL PERFORMERS IN THE WORLD TO HAVE THAT EXPERIENCE.
I HAVE A BAD HABIT OF BELIEVING THAT WHAT MAKES ME HAPPY...
...SHOULD MAKE OTHER PEOPLE HAPPY, TOO.
I HAD HOPED...
...THIS WOULD FIX MY RELATION-SHIP WITH MR. RIME AND ALSO SERVE AS A GOOD REMINDER TO ME.
UM...
I'M NOT DONE WITH THE CANE YET.

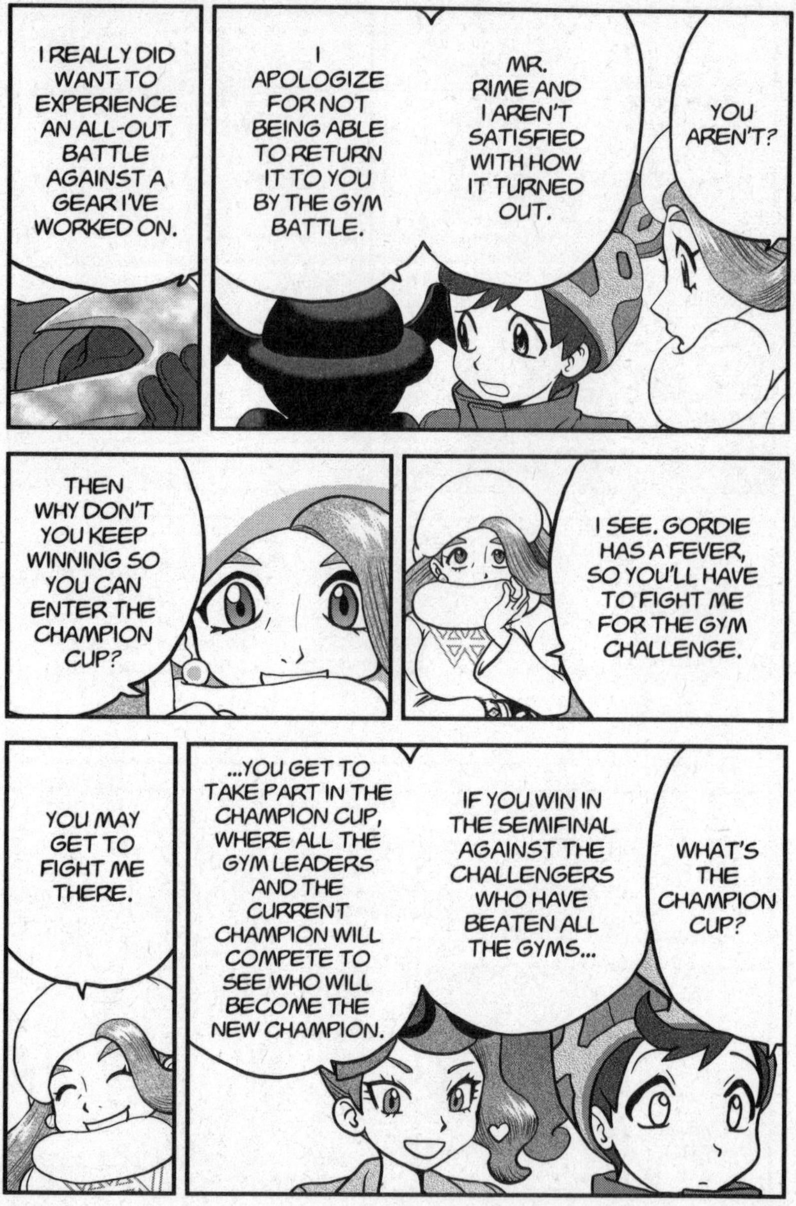
YOU AREN'T?
MR. RIME AND I AREN'T SATISFIED WITH HOW IT TURNED OUT.
I APOLOGIZE FOR NOT BEING ABLE TO RETURN IT TO YOU BY THE GYM BATTLE.
I REALLY DID WANT TO EXPERIENCE AN ALL-OUT BATTLE AGAINST A GEAR I'VE WORKED ON.
I SEE. GORDIE HAS A FEVER, SO YOU'LL HAVE TO FIGHT ME FOR THE GYM CHALLENGE.
THEN WHY DON'T YOU KEEP WINNING SO YOU CAN ENTER THE CHAMPION CUP?
WHAT'S THE CHAMPION CUP?
IF YOU WIN IN THE SEMIFINAL AGAINST THE CHALLENGERS WHO HAVE BEATEN ALL THE GYMS...
...YOU GET TO TAKE PART IN THE CHAMPION CUP, WHERE ALL THE GYM LEADERS AND THE CURRENT CHAMPION WILL COMPETE TO SEE WHO WILL BECOME THE NEW CHAMPION.
YOU MAY GET TO FIGHT ME THERE.

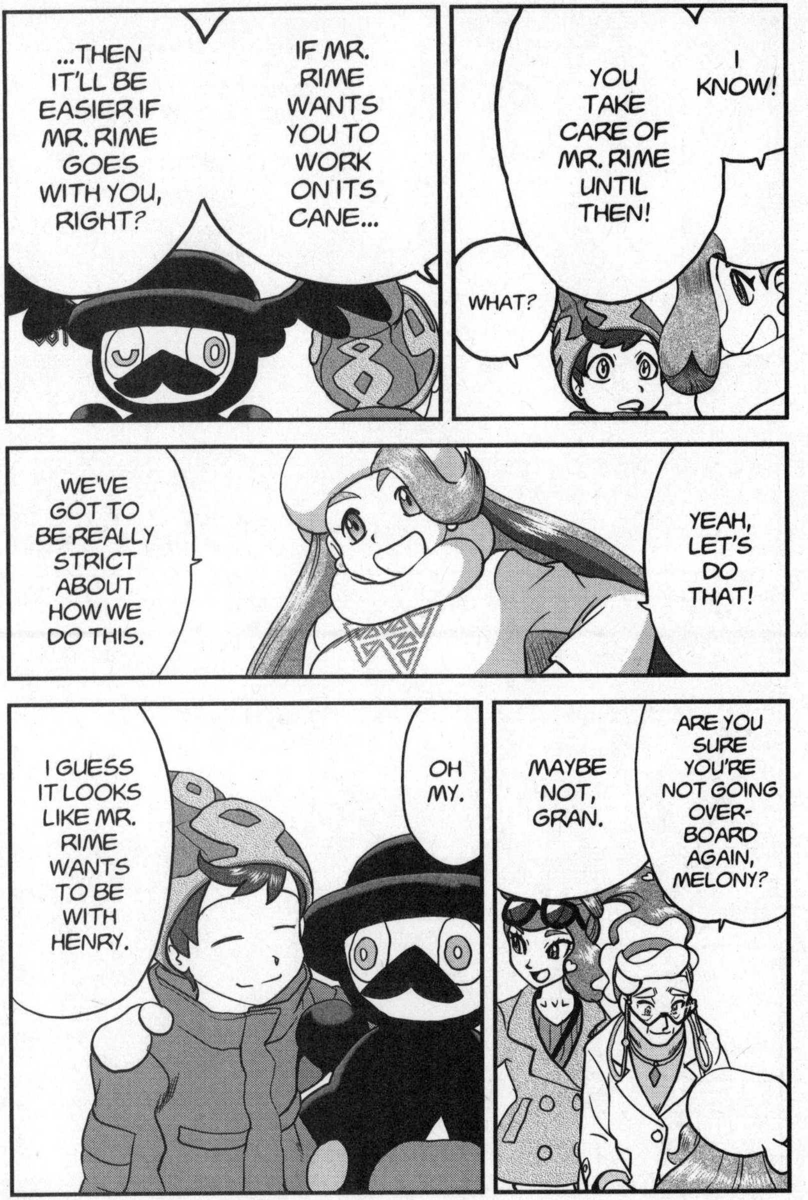
I KNOW!
YOU TAKE CARE OF MR. RIME UNTIL THEN!
WHAT?
IF MR. RIME WANTS YOU TO WORK ON ITS CANE...
...THEN IT'LL BE EASIER IF MR. RIME GOES WITH YOU, RIGHT?
YEAH, LET'S DO THAT!
WE'VE GOT TO BE REALLY STRICT ABOUT HOW WE DO THIS.
ARE YOU SURE YOU'RE NOT GOING OVER-BOARD AGAIN, MELONY?
MAYBE NOT, GRAN.
OH MY.
I GUESS IT LOOKS LIKE MR. RIME WANTS TO BE WITH HENRY.

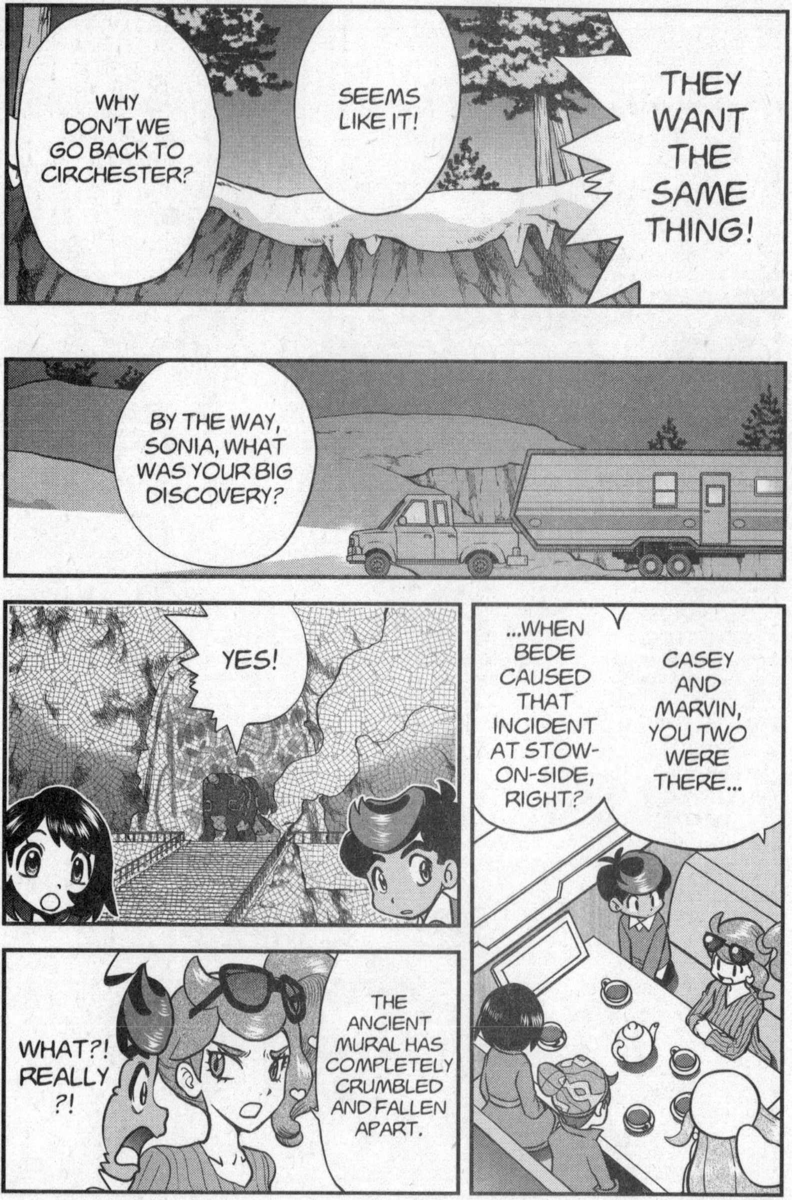
THEY WANT THE SAME THING!
SEEMS LIKE IT!
WHY DON'T WE GO BACK TO CIRCHESTER?
BY THE WAY, SONIA, WHAT WAS YOUR BIG DISCOVERY?
CASEY AND MARVIN, YOU TWO WERE THERE...
...WHEN BEDE CAUSED THAT INCIDENT AT STOW-ON-SIDE, RIGHT?
YES!
THE ANCIENT MURAL HAS COMPLETELY CRUMBLED AND FALLEN APART.
WHAT?! REALLY?!

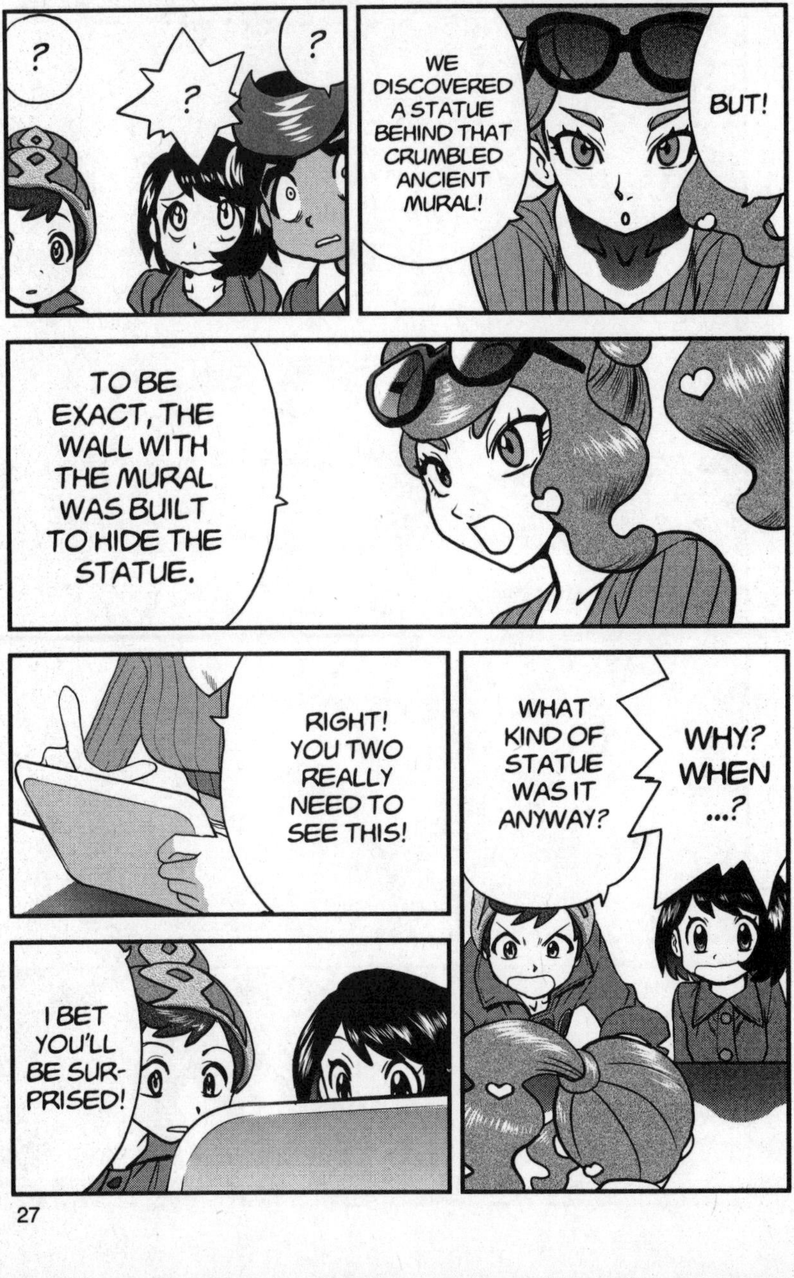
BUT!
WE DISCOVERED A STATUE BEHIND THAT CRUMBLED ANCIENT MURAL!
?
?
?
TO BE EXACT, THE WALL WITH THE MURAL WAS BUILT TO HIDE THE STATUE.
WHY? WHEN ...?
WHAT KIND OF STATUE WAS IT ANYWAY?
RIGHT! YOU TWO REALLY NEED TO SEE THIS!
I BET YOU'LL BE SUR-PRISED!

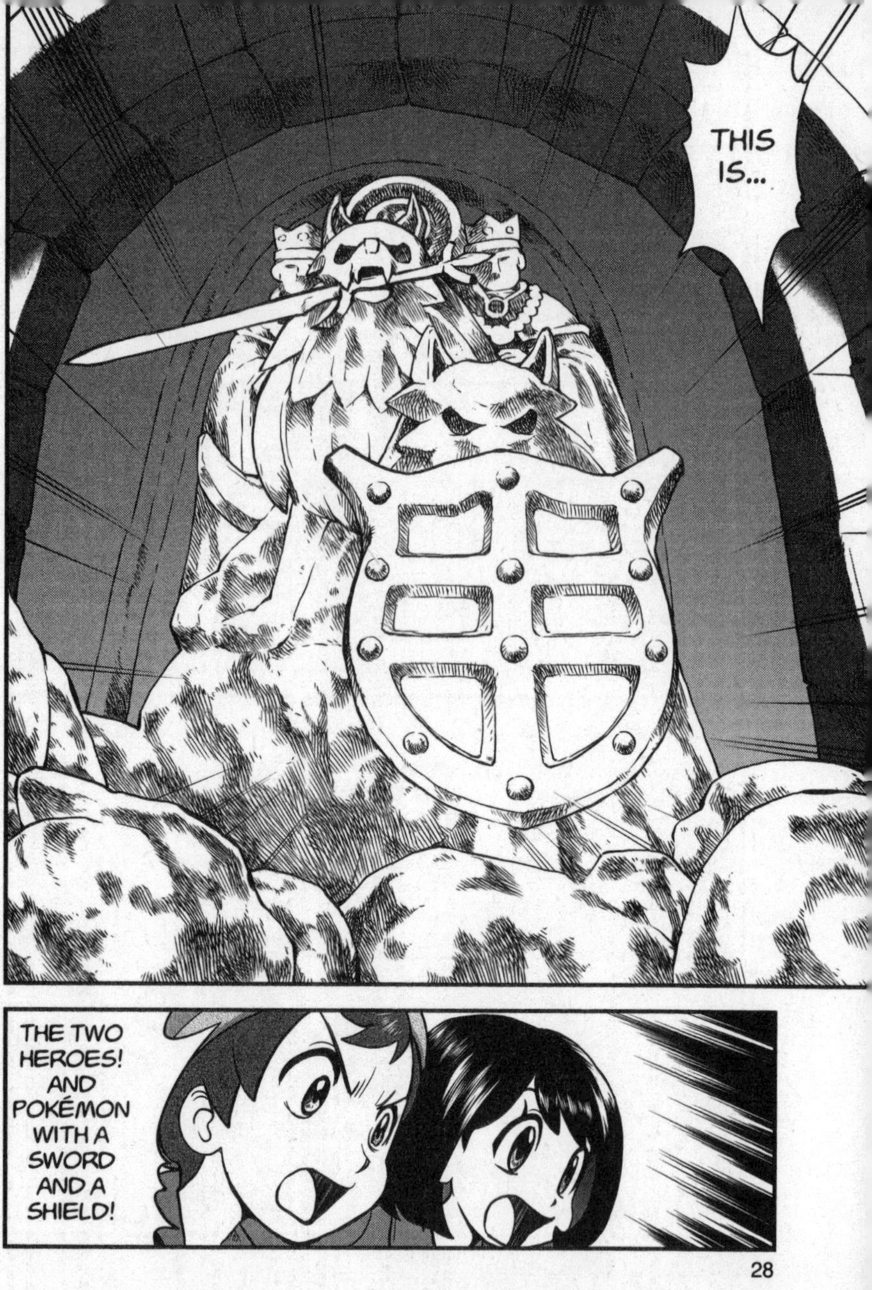
THIS IS...
THE TWO HEROES! AND POKÉMON WITH A SWORD AND A SHIELD!

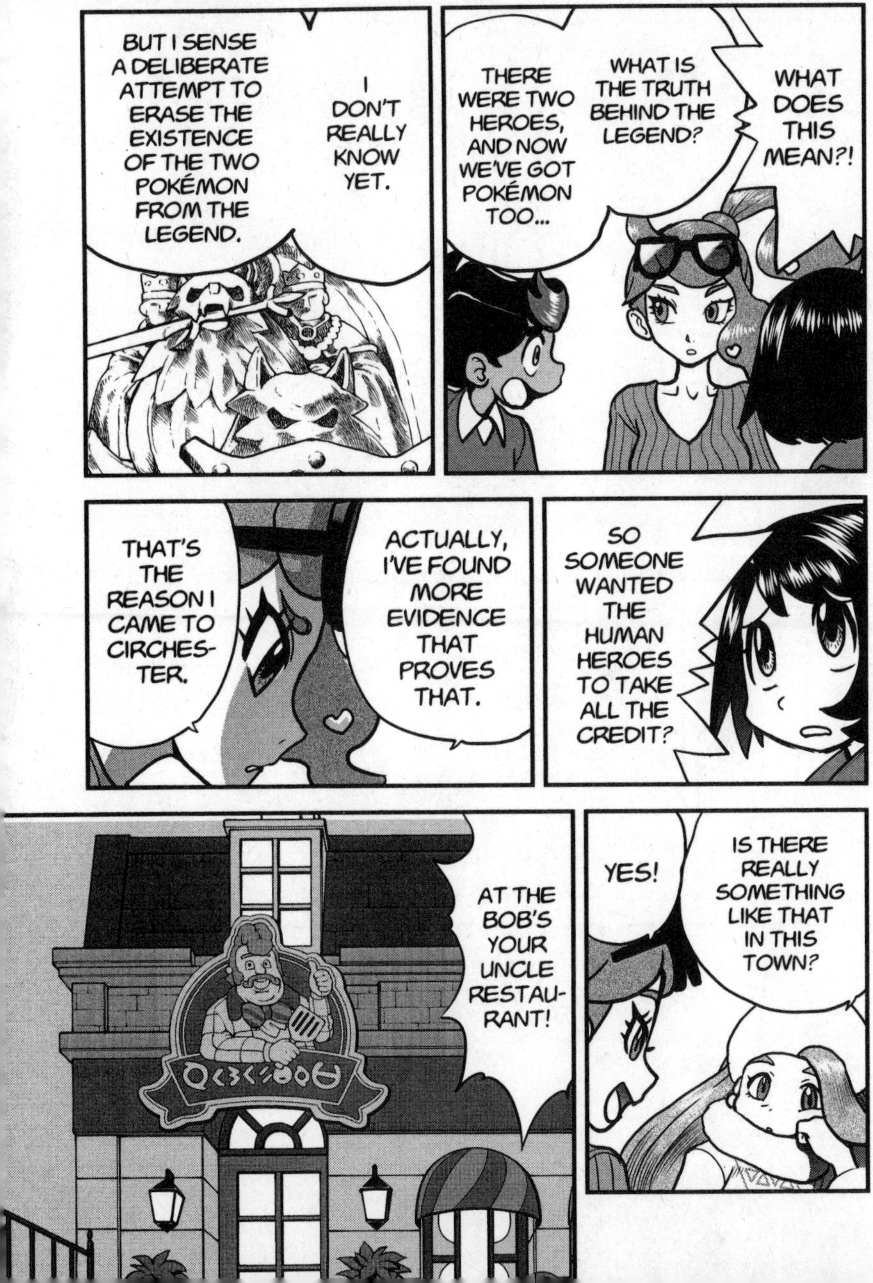
WHAT DOES THIS MEAN?!
WHAT IS THE TRUTH BEHIND THE LEGEND?
THERE WERE TWO HEROES, AND NOW WE'VE GOT POKÉMON TOO...
I DON'T REALLY KNOW YET.
BUT I SENSE A DELIBERATE ATTEMPT TO ERASE THE EXISTENCE OF THE TWO POKÉMON FROM THE LEGEND.
SO SOMEONE WANTED THE HUMAN HEROES TO TAKE ALL THE CREDIT?
ACTUALLY, I'VE FOUND MORE EVIDENCE THAT PROVES THAT.
THAT'S THE REASON I CAME TO CIRCHES-TER.
IS THERE REALLY SOMETHING LIKE THAT IN THIS TOWN?
YES!
AT THE BOB'S YOUR UNCLE RESTAU-RANT!

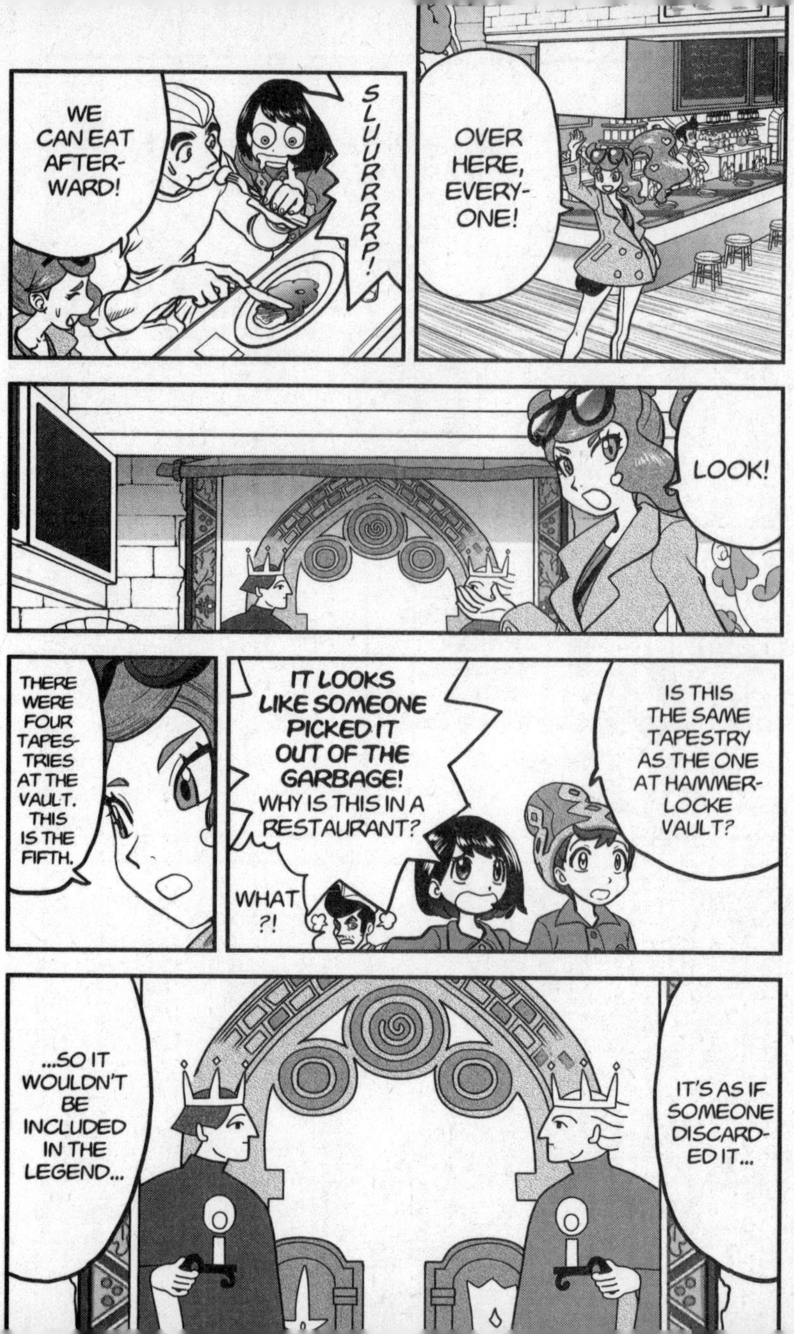
OVER HERE, EVERY-ONE!
SLUURRRRP!
WE CAN EAT AFTER-WARD!
LOOK!
IS THIS THE SAME TAPESTRY AS THE ONE AT HAMMER-LOCKE VAULT?
IT LOOKS LIKE SOMEONE PICKED IT OUT OF THE GARBAGE! WHY IS THIS IN A RESTAURANT?
WHAT ?!
THERE WERE FOUR TAPES-TRIES AT THE VAULT. THIS IS THE FIFTH.
IT'S AS IF SOMEONE DISCARD-ED IT...
...SO IT WOULDN'T BE INCLUDED IN THE LEGEND...

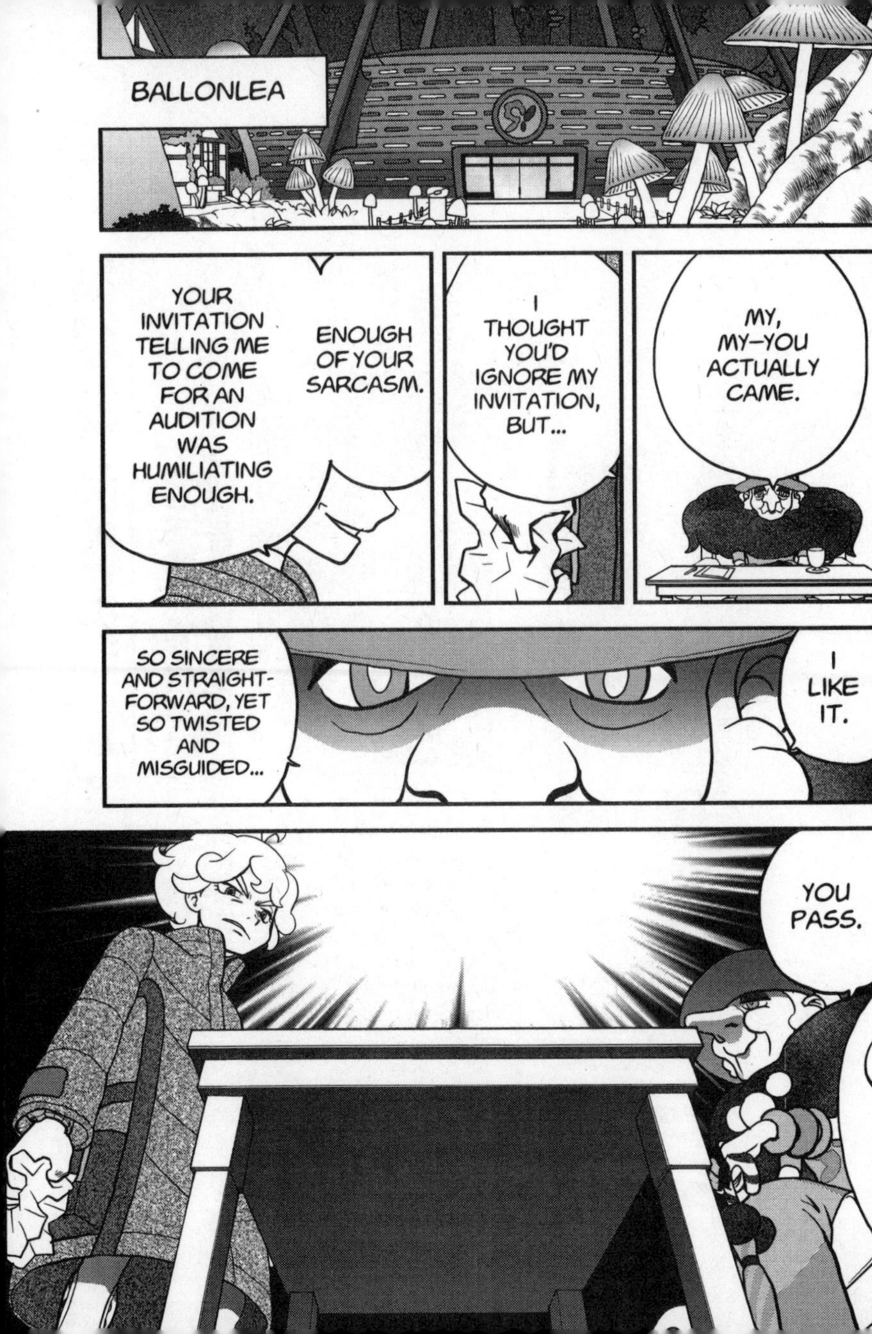
BALLONLEA
MY, MY—YOU ACTUALLY CAME.
I THOUGHT YOU'D IGNORE MY INVITATION, BUT...
ENOUGH OF YOUR SARCASM.
YOUR INVITATION TELLING ME TO COME FOR AN AUDITION WAS HUMILIATING ENOUGH.
I LIKE IT.
SO SINCERE AND STRAIGHT-FORWARD, YET SO TWISTED AND MISGUIDED...
YOU PASS.

GIGANTAMAX MACHAMP

TYPE:	Fighting
ABILITY:	Guts No Guard
G-MAX MOVE:	G-Max Chi Strike

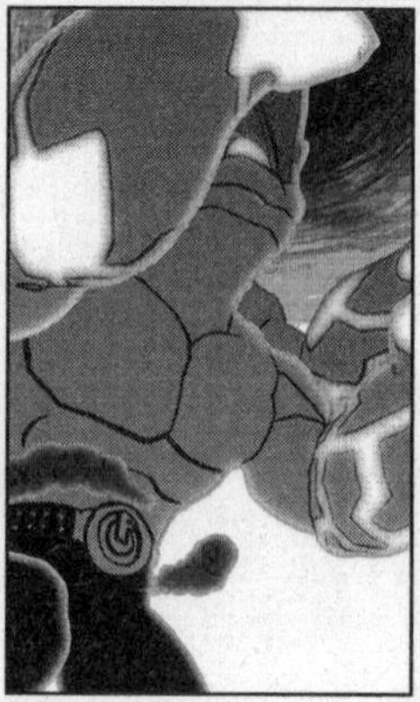

HEIGHT:	82'0"+
WEIGHT:	??? lbs

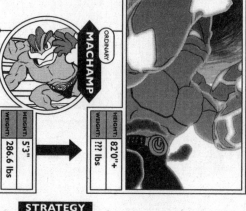

ORDINARY

MACHAMP

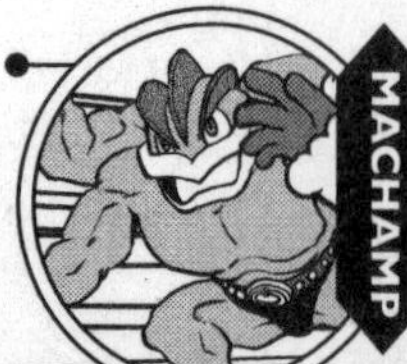

HEIGHT:	5'3"
WEIGHT:	286.6 lbs

Its bulky muscles have gotten even larger. One of these Pokémon once used its immeasurable strength to lift a capsizing ship and carry it safely to port. The glowing orange fists deliver explosive punches that knock out its opponent.

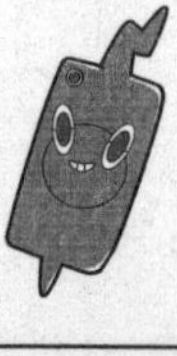

STRATEGY NOTES

The Fighting-type move used by a Gigantamax Machamp is G-Max Chi Strike. It increases the probability of a critical hit. It also increases the ability of allies to land a critical hit when it is used in a Raid Battle. Fight together and the Pokémon will do their best. Let's win this battle!

Adventure 21 Swaying!! Murky Memories

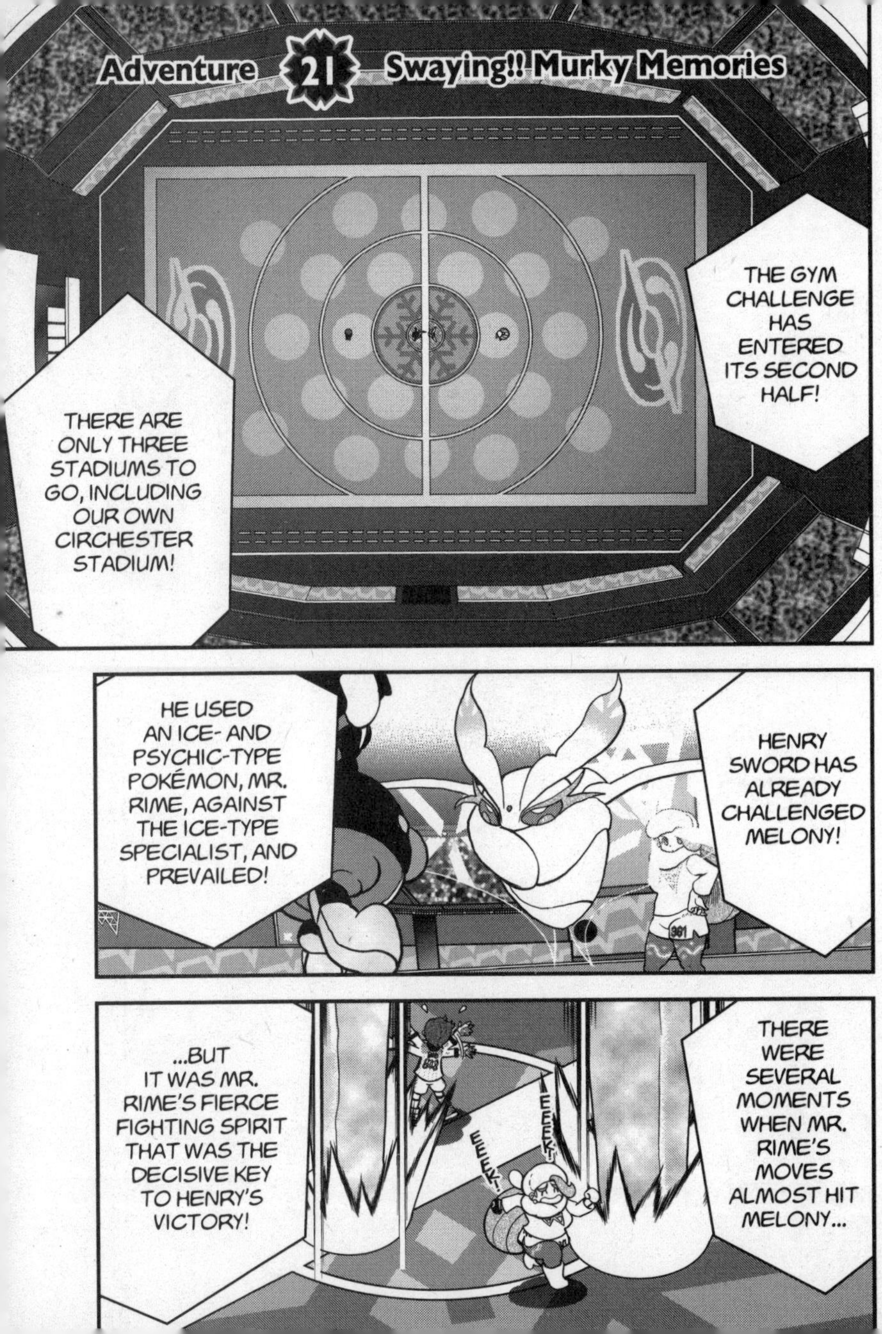
THE GYM CHALLENGE HAS ENTERED ITS SECOND HALF!
THERE ARE ONLY THREE STADIUMS TO GO, INCLUDING OUR OWN CIRCHESTER STADIUM!
HENRY SWORD HAS ALREADY CHALLENGED MELONY!
HE USED AN ICE- AND PSYCHIC-TYPE POKÉMON, MR. RIME, AGAINST THE ICE-TYPE SPECIALIST, AND PREVAILED!
THERE WERE SEVERAL MOMENTS WHEN MR. RIME'S MOVES ALMOST HIT MELONY...
EEEEK!
EEEK!
...BUT IT WAS MR. RIME'S FIERCE FIGHTING SPIRIT THAT WAS THE DECISIVE KEY TO HENRY'S VICTORY!

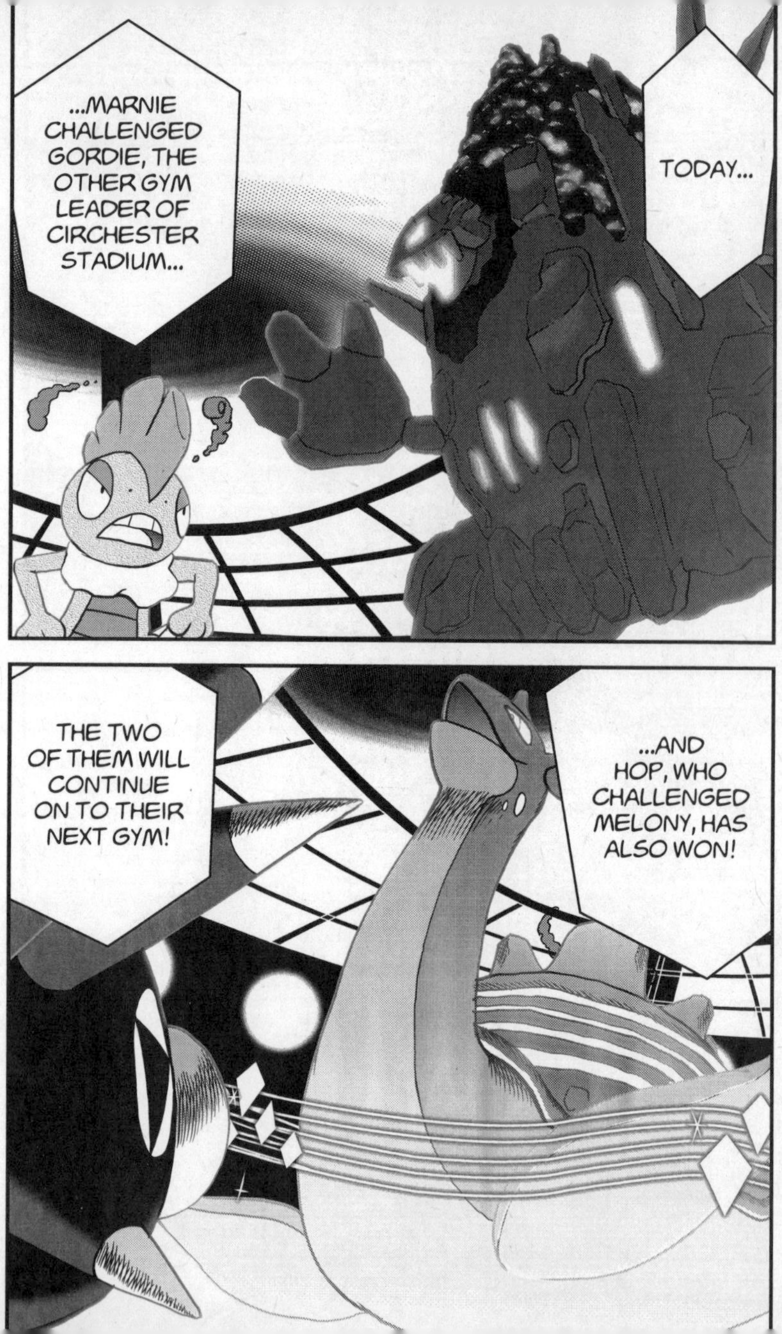
TODAY...
...MARNIE CHALLENGED GORDIE, THE OTHER GYM LEADER OF CIRCHESTER STADIUM...
...AND HOP, WHO CHALLENGED MELONY, HAS ALSO WON!
THE TWO OF THEM WILL CONTINUE ON TO THEIR NEXT GYM!

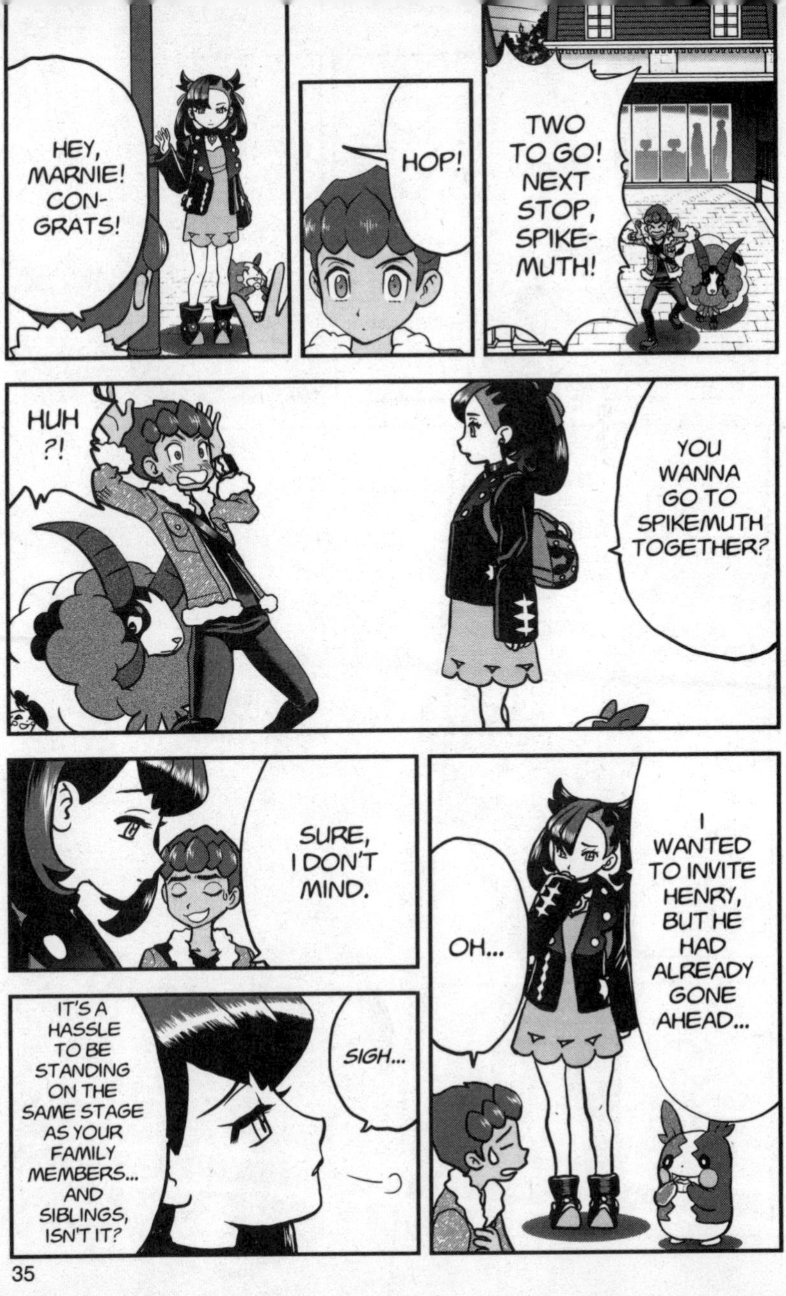
TWO TO GO! NEXT STOP, SPIKE-MUTH!
HOP!
HEY, MARNIE! CON-GRATS!
YOU WANNA GO TO SPIKEMUTH TOGETHER?
HUH ?!
I WANTED TO INVITE HENRY, BUT HE HAD ALREADY GONE AHEAD...
OH...
SURE, I DON'T MIND.
SIGH...
IT'S A HASSLE TO BE STANDING ON THE SAME STAGE AS YOUR FAMILY MEMBERS... AND SIBLINGS, ISN'T IT?

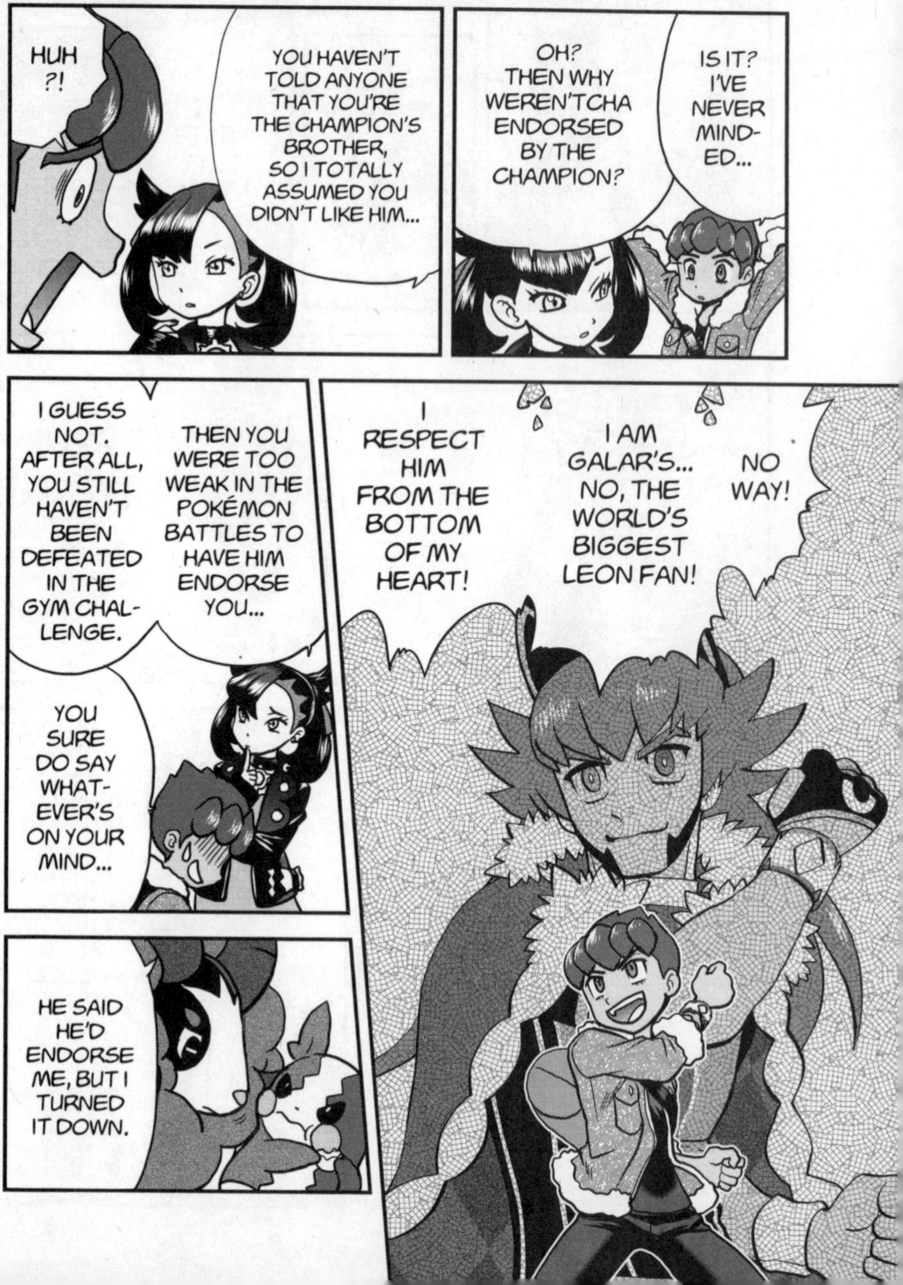
IS IT? I'VE NEVER MIND-ED...
OH? THEN WHY WEREN'TCHA ENDORSED BY THE CHAMPION?
YOU HAVEN'T TOLD ANYONE THAT YOU'RE THE CHAMPION'S BROTHER, SO I TOTALLY ASSUMED YOU DIDN'T LIKE HIM...
HUH ?!
NO WAY!
I AM GALAR'S... NO, THE WORLD'S BIGGEST LEON FAN!
I RESPECT HIM FROM THE BOTTOM OF MY HEART!
THEN YOU WERE TOO WEAK IN THE POKÉMON BATTLES TO HAVE HIM ENDORSE YOU...
I GUESS NOT. AFTER ALL, YOU STILL HAVEN'T BEEN DEFEATED IN THE GYM CHAL-LENGE.
YOU SURE DO SAY WHAT-EVER'S ON YOUR MIND...
HE SAID HE'D ENDORSE ME, BUT I TURNED IT DOWN.

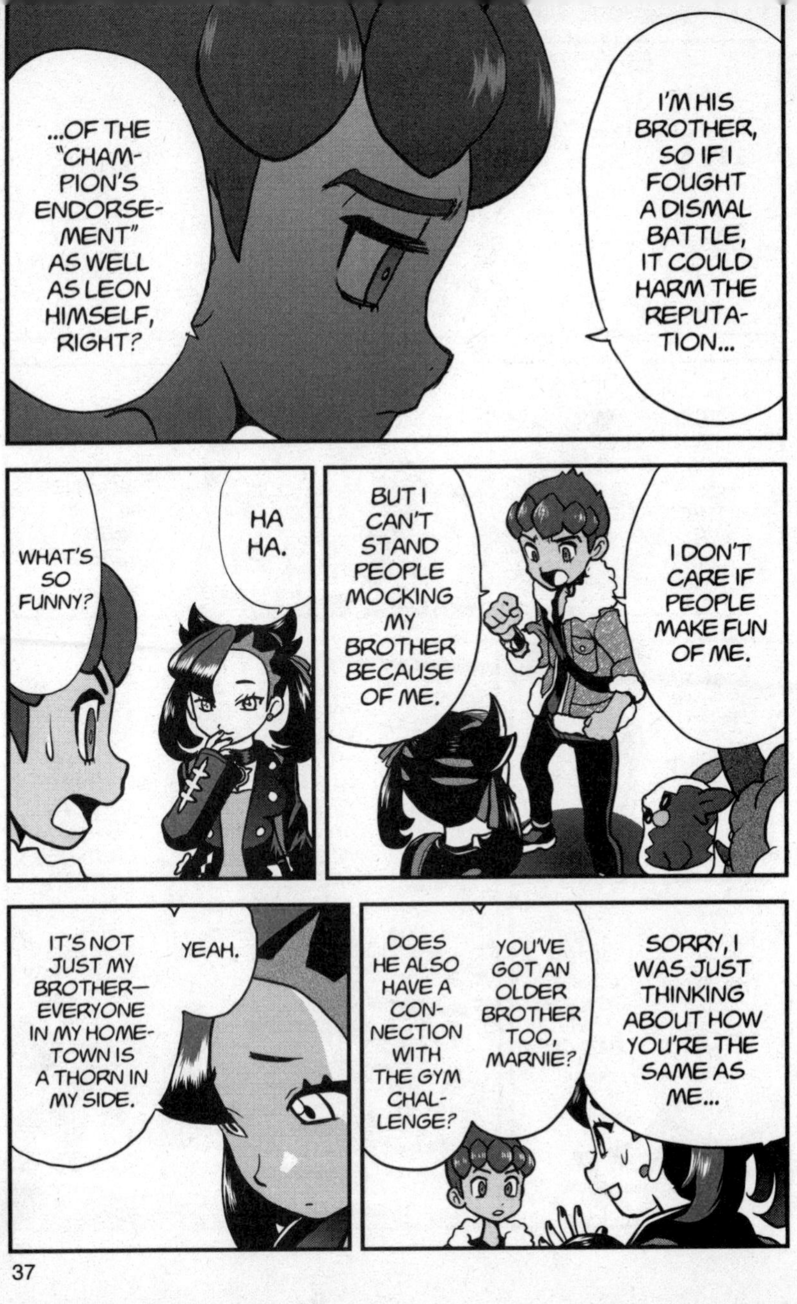
I'M HIS BROTHER, SO IF I FOUGHT A DISMAL BATTLE, IT COULD HARM THE REPUTATION...
...OF THE "CHAMPION'S ENDORSEMENT" AS WELL AS LEON HIMSELF, RIGHT?
I DON'T CARE IF PEOPLE MAKE FUN OF ME.
BUT I CAN'T STAND PEOPLE MOCKING MY BROTHER BECAUSE OF ME.
HA HA.
WHAT'S SO FUNNY?
SORRY, I WAS JUST THINKING ABOUT HOW YOU'RE THE SAME AS ME...
YOU'VE GOT AN OLDER BROTHER TOO, MARNIE?
DOES HE ALSO HAVE A CONNECTION WITH THE GYM CHALLENGE?
YEAH.
IT'S NOT JUST MY BROTHER—EVERYONE IN MY HOMETOWN IS A THORN IN MY SIDE.

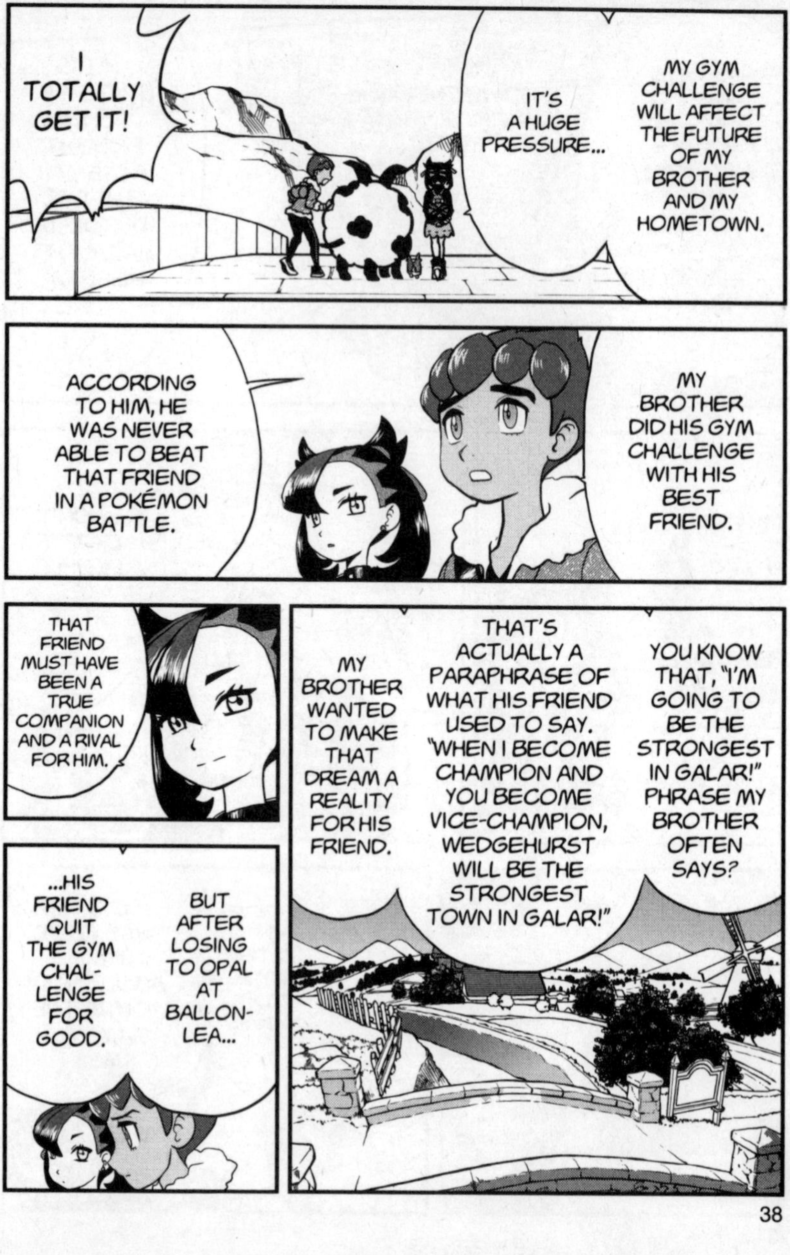
MY GYM CHALLENGE WILL AFFECT THE FUTURE OF MY BROTHER AND MY HOMETOWN.
IT'S A HUGE PRESSURE...
I TOTALLY GET IT!
MY BROTHER DID HIS GYM CHALLENGE WITH HIS BEST FRIEND.
ACCORDING TO HIM, HE WAS NEVER ABLE TO BEAT THAT FRIEND IN A POKÉMON BATTLE.
YOU KNOW THAT, "I'M GOING TO BE THE STRONGEST IN GALAR!" PHRASE MY BROTHER OFTEN SAYS?
THAT'S ACTUALLY A PARAPHRASE OF WHAT HIS FRIEND USED TO SAY. "WHEN I BECOME CHAMPION AND YOU BECOME VICE-CHAMPION, WEDGEHURST WILL BE THE STRONGEST TOWN IN GALAR!"
MY BROTHER WANTED TO MAKE THAT DREAM A REALITY FOR HIS FRIEND.
THAT FRIEND MUST HAVE BEEN A TRUE COMPANION AND A RIVAL FOR HIM.
BUT AFTER LOSING TO OPAL AT BALLON-LEA...
...HIS FRIEND QUIT THE GYM CHAL-LENGE FOR GOOD.

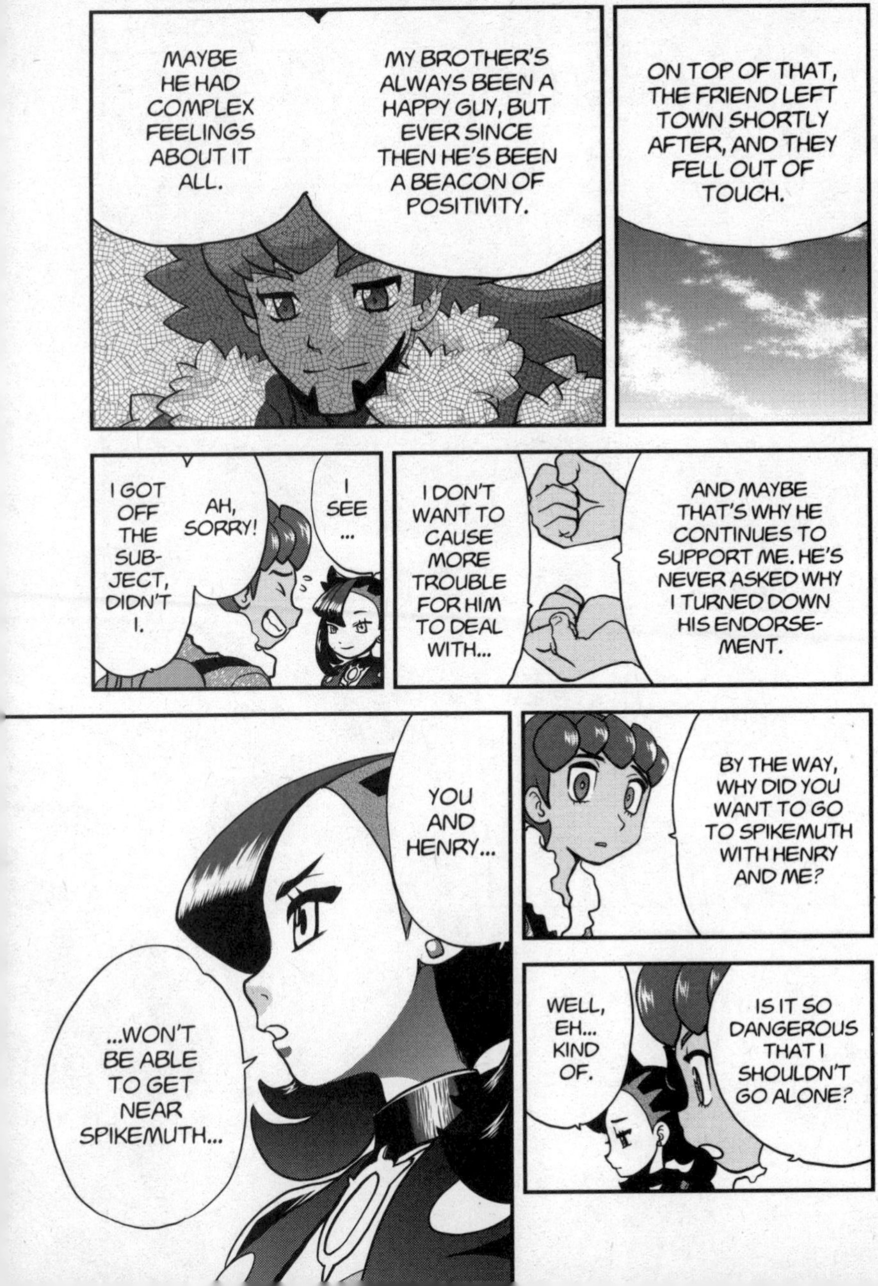
ON TOP OF THAT, THE FRIEND LEFT TOWN SHORTLY AFTER, AND THEY FELL OUT OF TOUCH.
MY BROTHER'S ALWAYS BEEN A HAPPY GUY, BUT EVER SINCE THEN HE'S BEEN A BEACON OF POSITIVITY.
MAYBE HE HAD COMPLEX FEELINGS ABOUT IT ALL.
AND MAYBE THAT'S WHY HE CONTINUES TO SUPPORT ME. HE'S NEVER ASKED WHY I TURNED DOWN HIS ENDORSE-MENT.
I DON'T WANT TO CAUSE MORE TROUBLE FOR HIM TO DEAL WITH...
I SEE ...
AH, SORRY!
I GOT OFF THE SUB-JECT, DIDN'T I.
BY THE WAY, WHY DID YOU WANT TO GO TO SPIKEMUTH WITH HENRY AND ME?
IS IT SO DANGEROUS THAT I SHOULDN'T GO ALONE?
WELL, EH... KIND OF.
YOU AND HENRY...
...WON'T BE ABLE TO GET NEAR SPIKEMUTH...

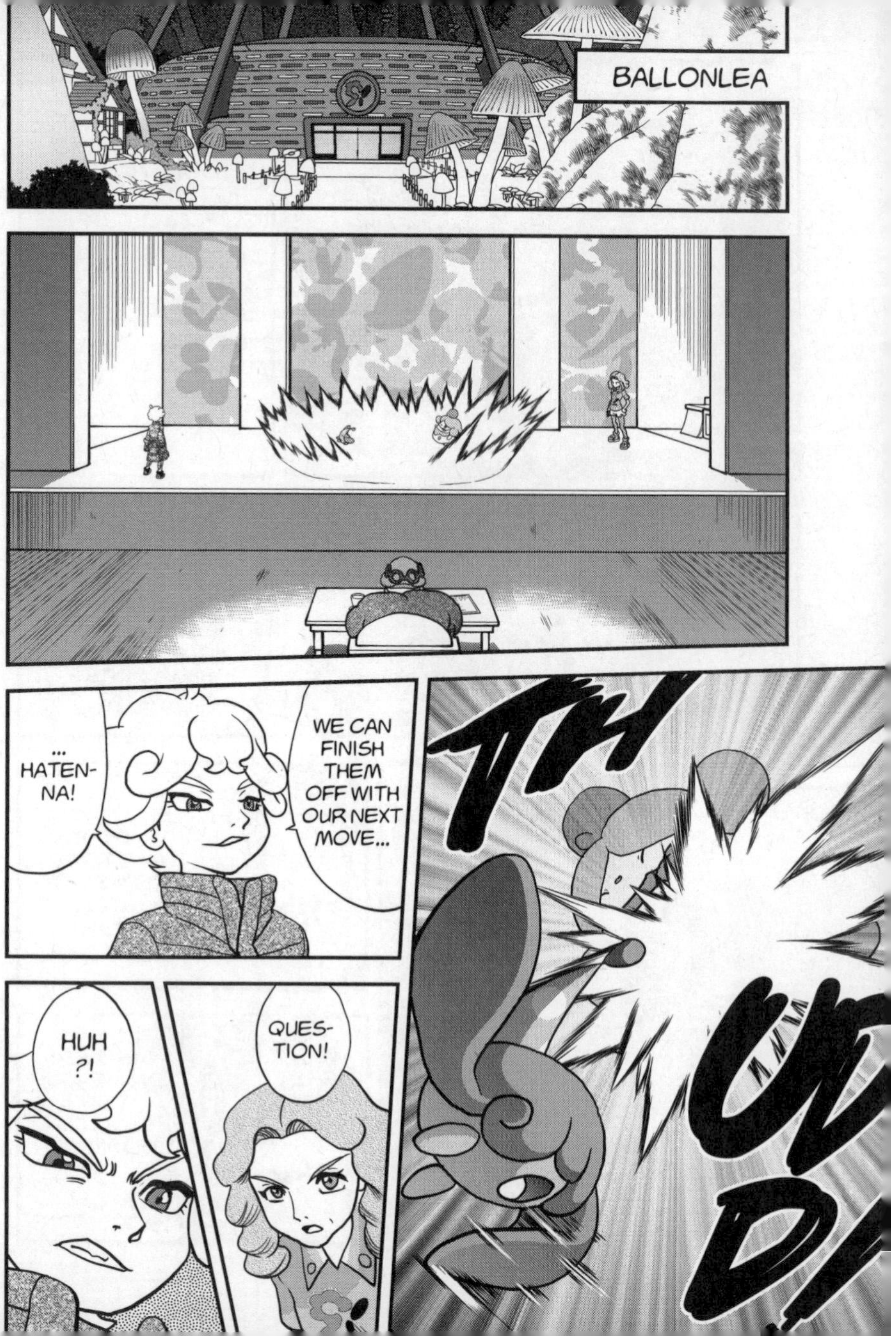
BALLONLEA
WE CAN FINISH THEM OFF WITH OUR NEXT MOVE...
... HATEN-NA!
QUES-TION!
HUH?!

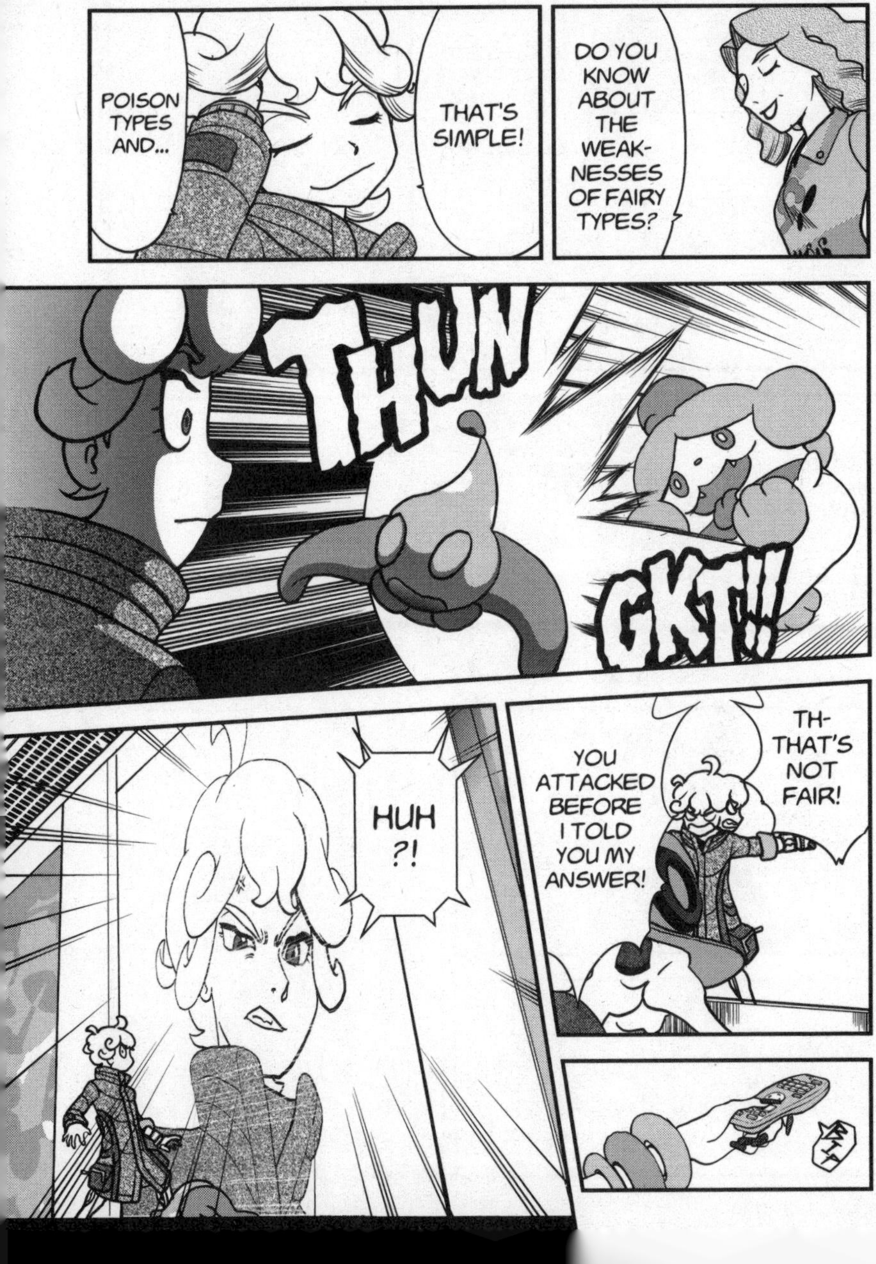
DO YOU KNOW ABOUT THE WEAKNESSES OF FAIRY TYPES?
THAT'S SIMPLE!
POISON TYPES AND...
THUN
GKT!!
TH- THAT'S NOT FAIR!
YOU ATTACKED BEFORE I TOLD YOU MY ANSWER!
HUH ?!

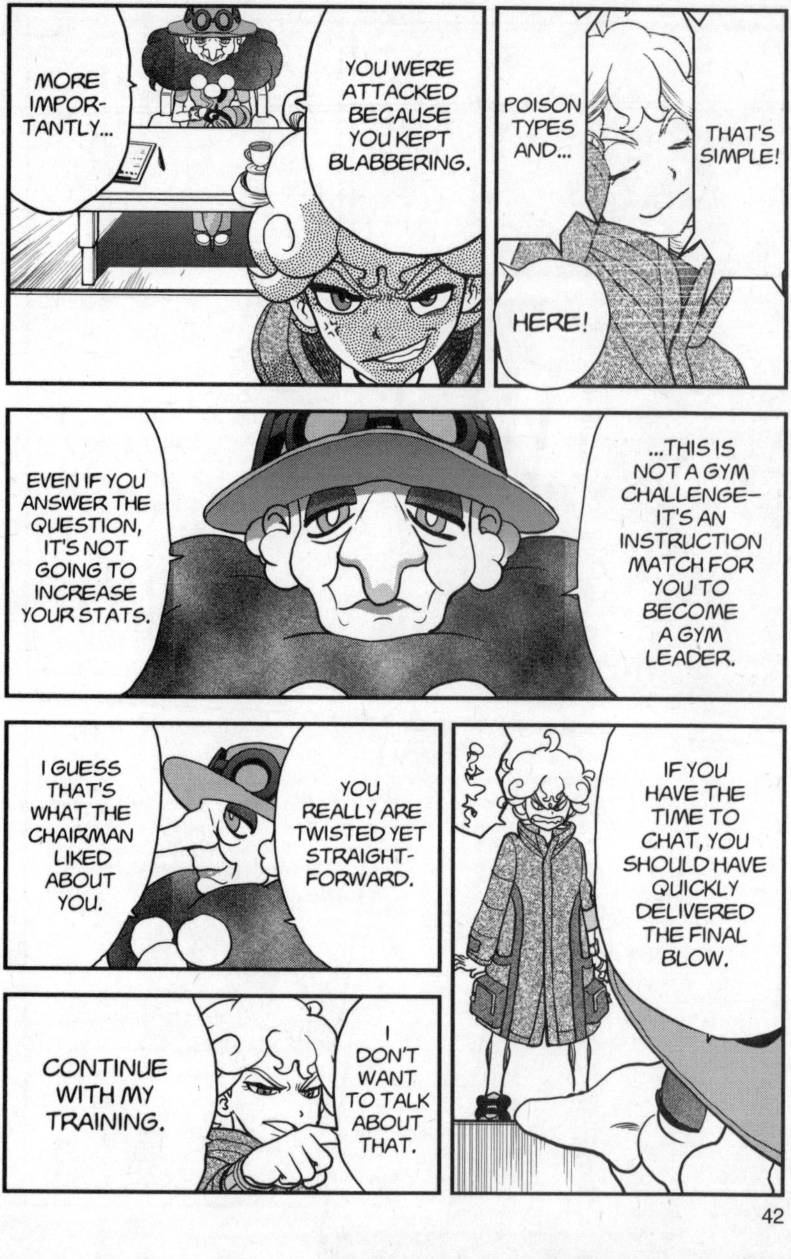
THAT'S SIMPLE!
POISON TYPES AND...
HERE!
YOU WERE ATTACKED BECAUSE YOU KEPT BLABBERING.
MORE IMPORTANTLY...
...THIS IS NOT A GYM CHALLENGE— IT'S AN INSTRUCTION MATCH FOR YOU TO BECOME A GYM LEADER.
EVEN IF YOU ANSWER THE QUESTION, IT'S NOT GOING TO INCREASE YOUR STATS.
IF YOU HAVE THE TIME TO CHAT, YOU SHOULD HAVE QUICKLY DELIVERED THE FINAL BLOW.
YOU REALLY ARE TWISTED YET STRAIGHT-FORWARD.
I GUESS THAT'S WHAT THE CHAIRMAN LIKED ABOUT YOU.
I DON'T WANT TO TALK ABOUT THAT.
CONTINUE WITH MY TRAINING.

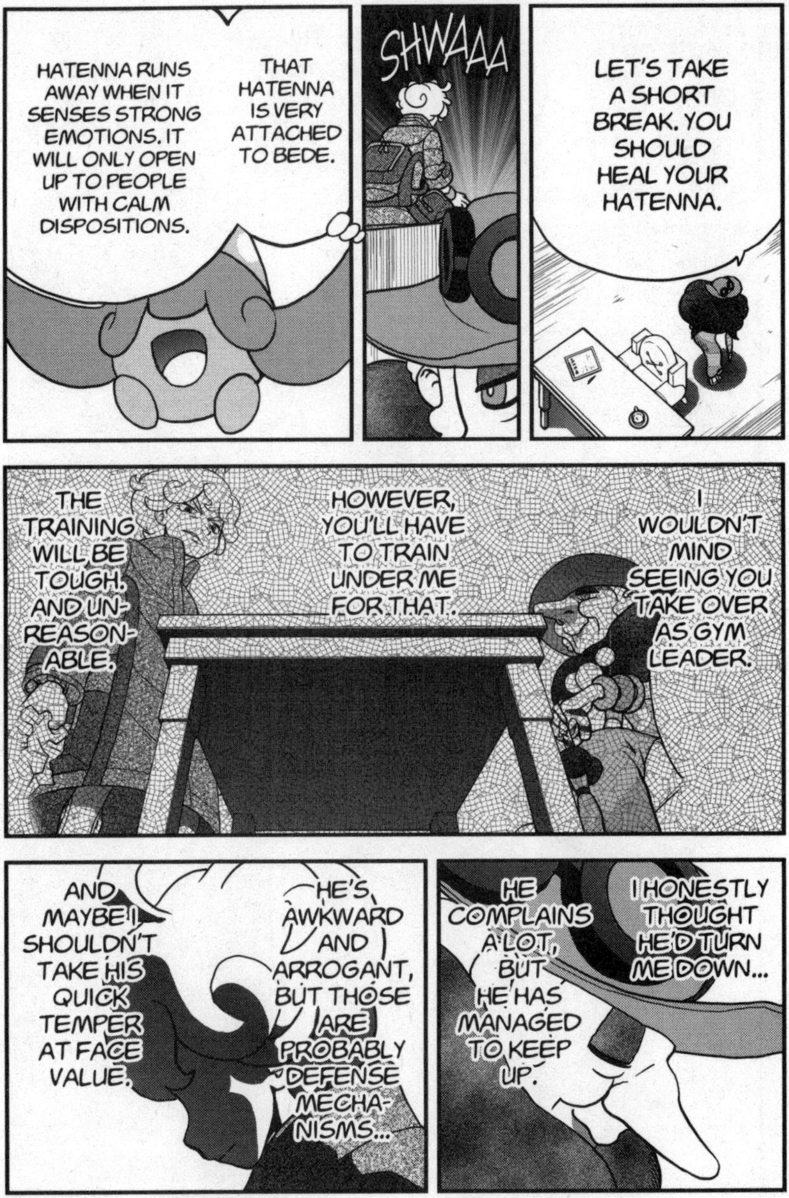
LET'S TAKE A SHORT BREAK. YOU SHOULD HEAL YOUR HATENNA.
SHWAAA
THAT HATENNA IS VERY ATTACHED TO BEDE.
HATENNA RUNS AWAY WHEN IT SENSES STRONG EMOTIONS. IT WILL ONLY OPEN UP TO PEOPLE WITH CALM DISPOSITIONS.
I WOULDN'T MIND SEEING YOU TAKE OVER AS GYM LEADER.
HOWEVER, YOU'LL HAVE TO TRAIN UNDER ME FOR THAT.
THE TRAINING WILL BE TOUGH. AND UN-REASON-ABLE.
I HONESTLY THOUGHT HE'D TURN ME DOWN...
HE COMPLAINS A LOT, BUT HE HAS MANAGED TO KEEP UP.
HE'S AWKWARD AND ARROGANT, BUT THOSE ARE PROBABLY DEFENSE MECHA-NISMS...
AND MAYBE I SHOULDN'T TAKE HIS QUICK TEMPER AT FACE VALUE.

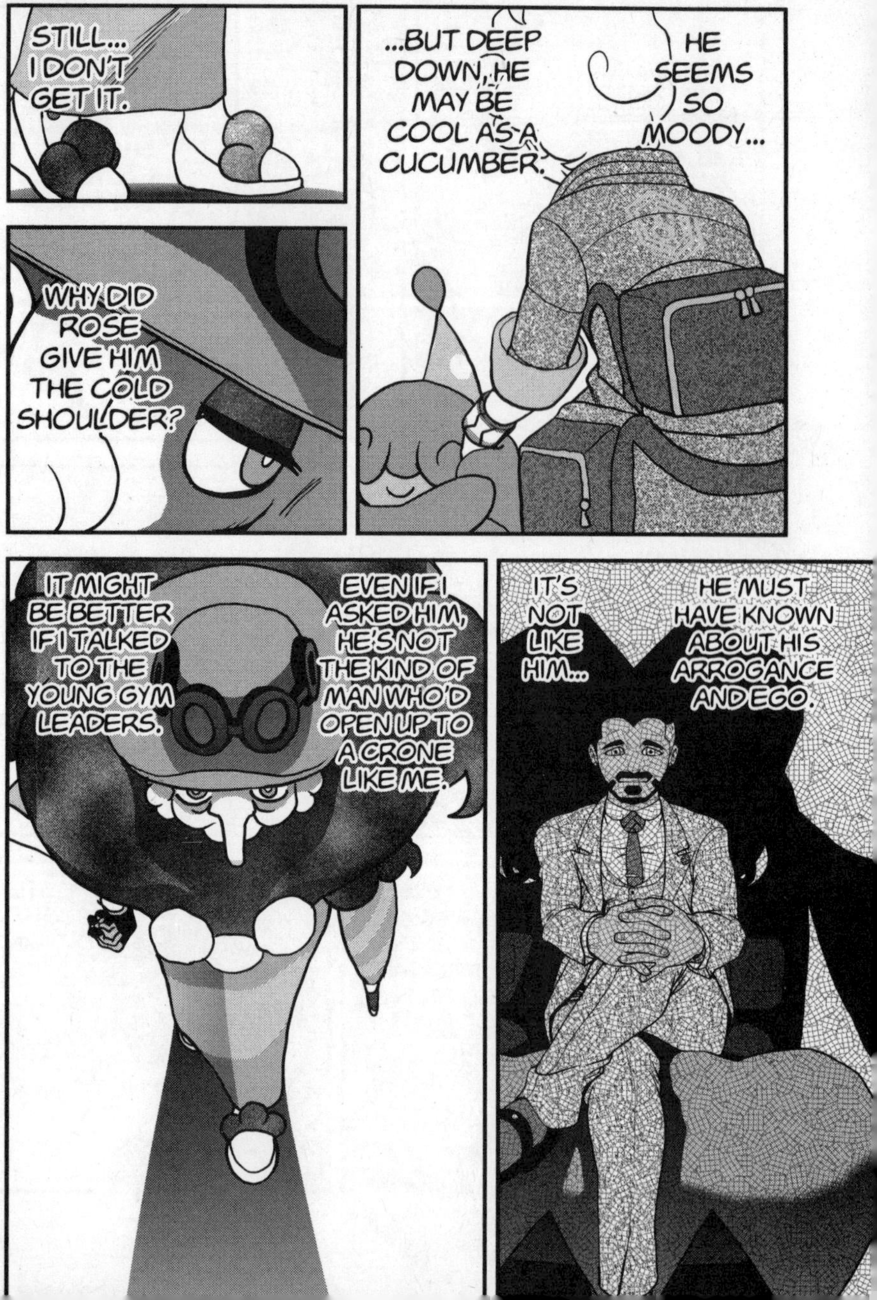
HE SEEMS SO MOODY...
...BUT DEEP DOWN, HE MAY BE COOL AS A CUCUMBER.
STILL... I DON'T GET IT.
WHY DID ROSE GIVE HIM THE COLD SHOULDER?
HE MUST HAVE KNOWN ABOUT HIS ARROGANCE AND EGO.
IT'S NOT LIKE HIM...
EVEN IF I ASKED HIM, HE'S NOT THE KIND OF MAN WHO'D OPEN UP TO A CRONE LIKE ME.
IT MIGHT BE BETTER IF I TALKED TO THE YOUNG GYM LEADERS.

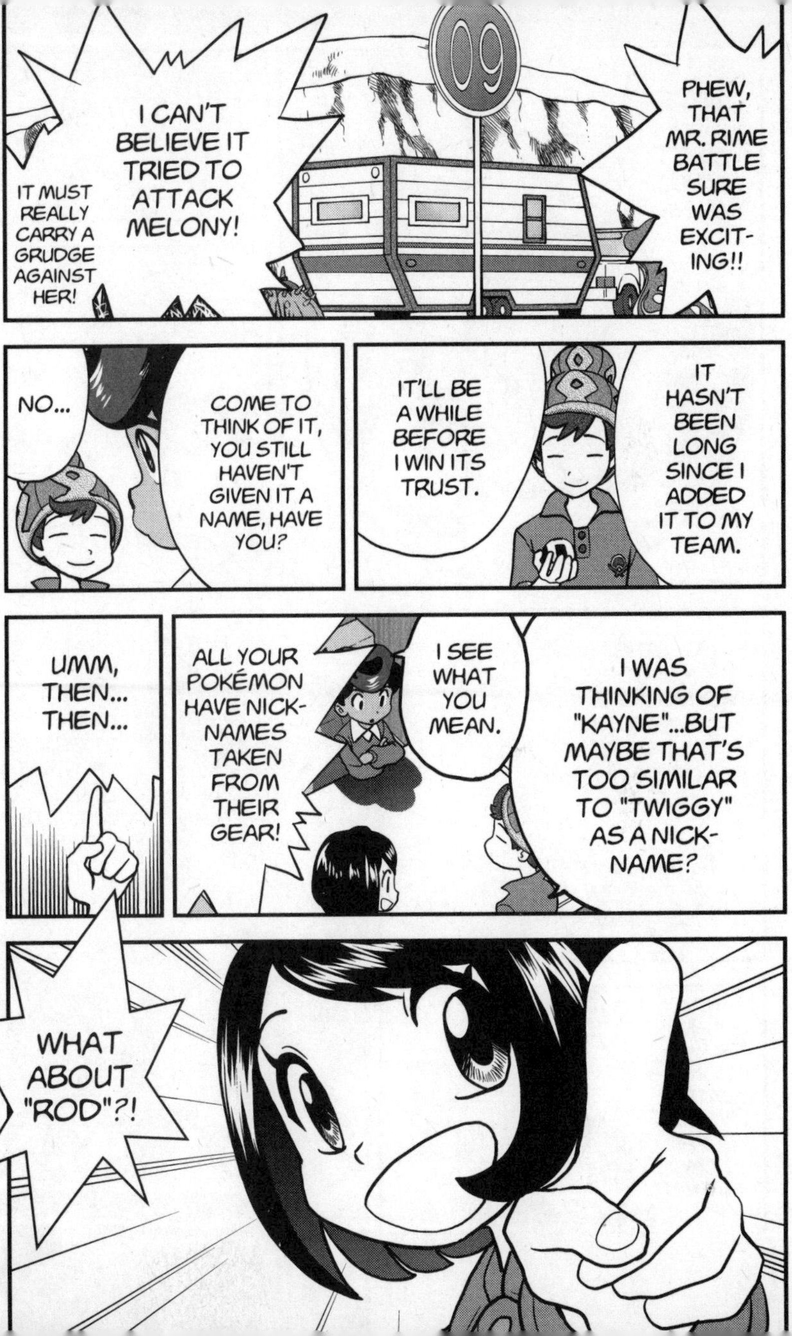
PHEW, THAT MR. RIME BATTLE SURE WAS EXCIT-ING!!
I CAN'T BELIEVE IT TRIED TO ATTACK MELONY!
IT MUST REALLY CARRY A GRUDGE AGAINST HER!
IT HASN'T BEEN LONG SINCE I ADDED IT TO MY TEAM.
IT'LL BE A WHILE BEFORE I WIN ITS TRUST.
COME TO THINK OF IT, YOU STILL HAVEN'T GIVEN IT A NAME, HAVE YOU?
NO...
I WAS THINKING OF "KAYNE"...BUT MAYBE THAT'S TOO SIMILAR TO "TWIGGY" AS A NICK-NAME?
I SEE WHAT YOU MEAN.
ALL YOUR POKÉMON HAVE NICK-NAMES TAKEN FROM THEIR GEAR!
UMM, THEN... THEN...
WHAT ABOUT "ROD"?!

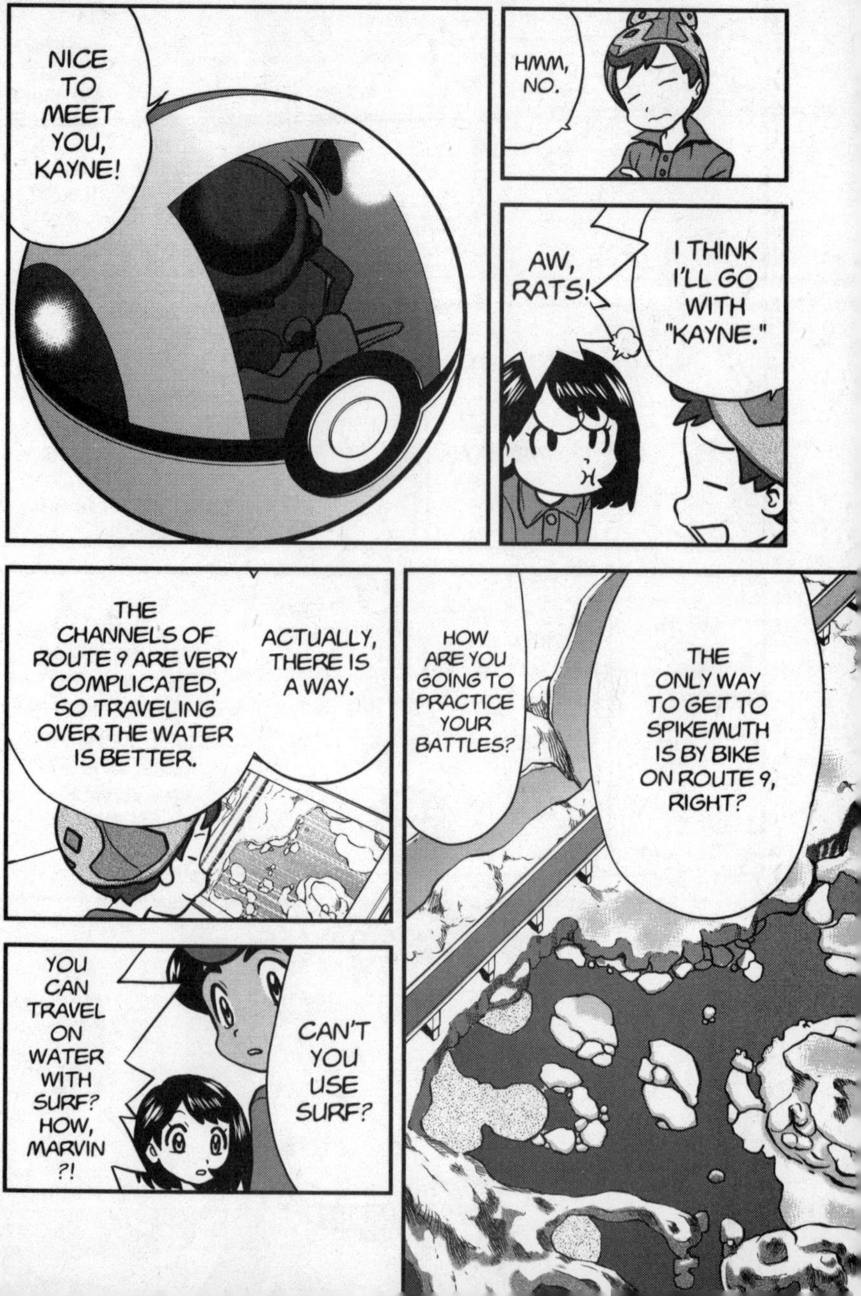
HMM, NO.
I THINK I'LL GO WITH "KAYNE."
AW, RATS!
NICE TO MEET YOU, KAYNE!
THE ONLY WAY TO GET TO SPIKEMUTH IS BY BIKE ON ROUTE 9, RIGHT?
HOW ARE YOU GOING TO PRACTICE YOUR BATTLES?
ACTUALLY, THERE IS A WAY.
THE CHANNELS OF ROUTE 9 ARE VERY COMPLICATED, SO TRAVELING OVER THE WATER IS BETTER.
CAN'T YOU USE SURF?
YOU CAN TRAVEL ON WATER WITH SURF? HOW, MARVIN ?!

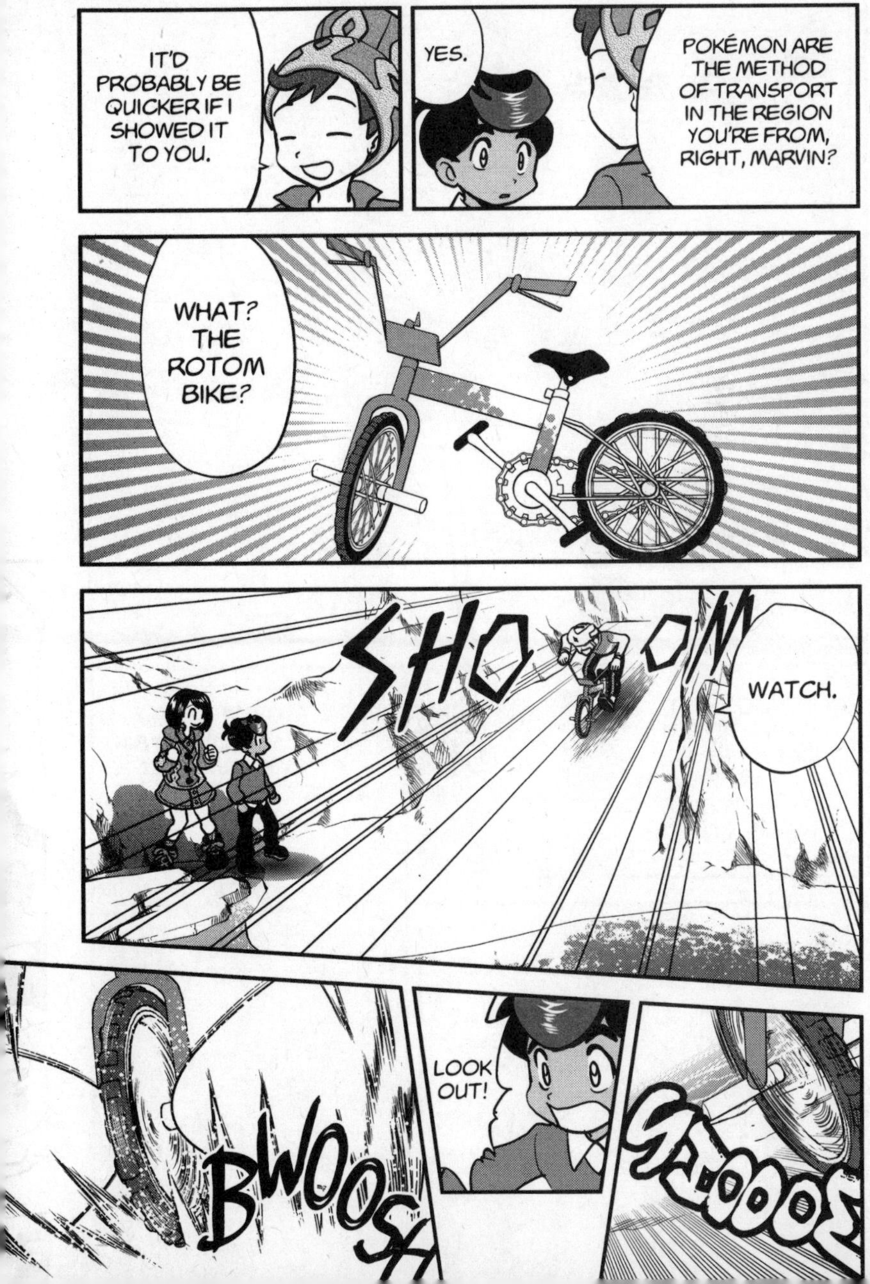
POKÉMON ARE THE METHOD OF TRANSPORT IN THE REGION YOU'RE FROM, RIGHT, MARVIN?
YES.
IT'D PROBABLY BE QUICKER IF I SHOWED IT TO YOU.
WHAT? THE ROTOM BIKE?
WATCH.
SHOOM
LOOK OUT!
BWOOSH

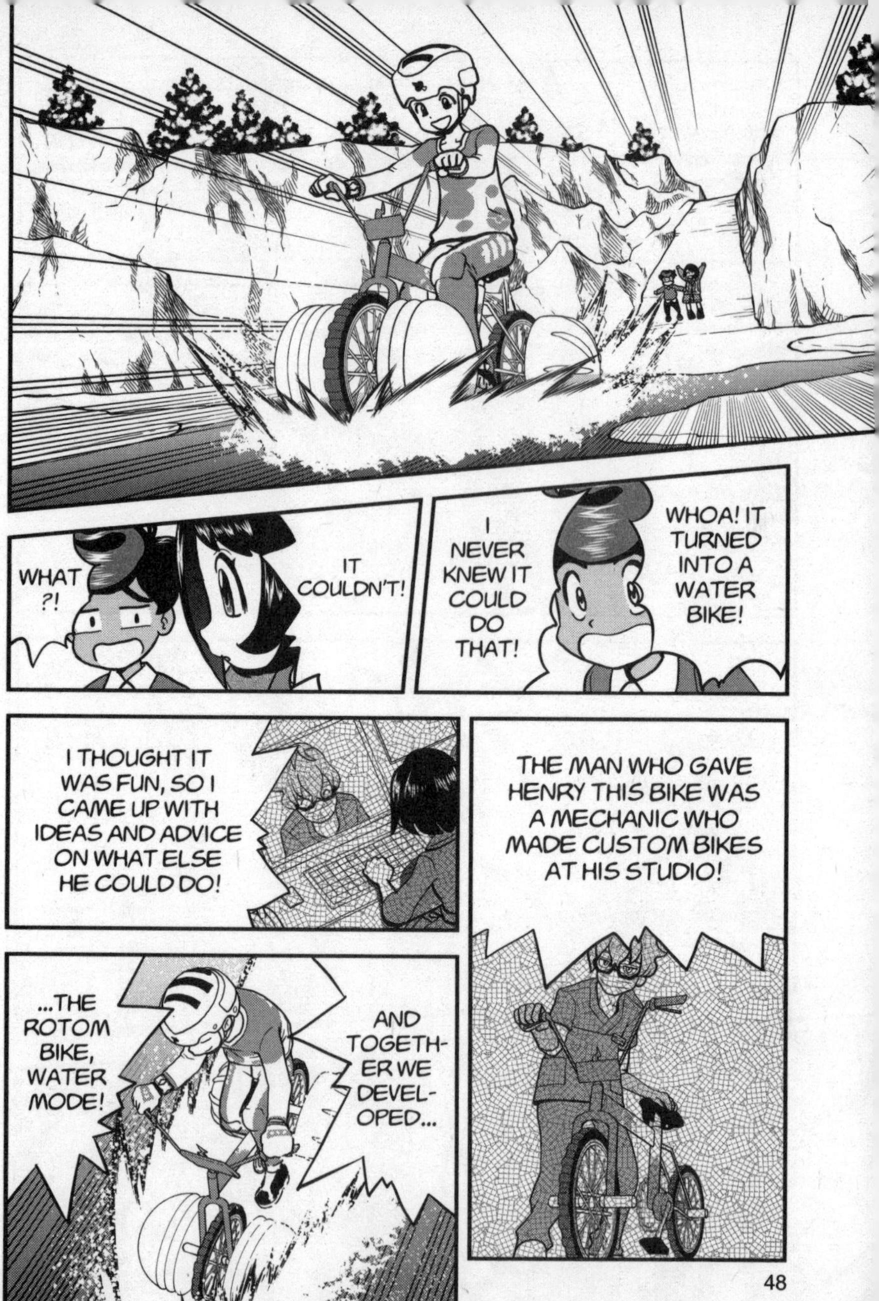
WHOA! IT TURNED INTO A WATER BIKE!
I NEVER KNEW IT COULD DO THAT!
IT COULDN'T!
WHAT?!
THE MAN WHO GAVE HENRY THIS BIKE WAS A MECHANIC WHO MADE CUSTOM BIKES AT HIS STUDIO!
I THOUGHT IT WAS FUN, SO I CAME UP WITH IDEAS AND ADVICE ON WHAT ELSE HE COULD DO!
AND TOGETHER WE DEVELOPED...
...THE ROTOM BIKE, WATER MODE!

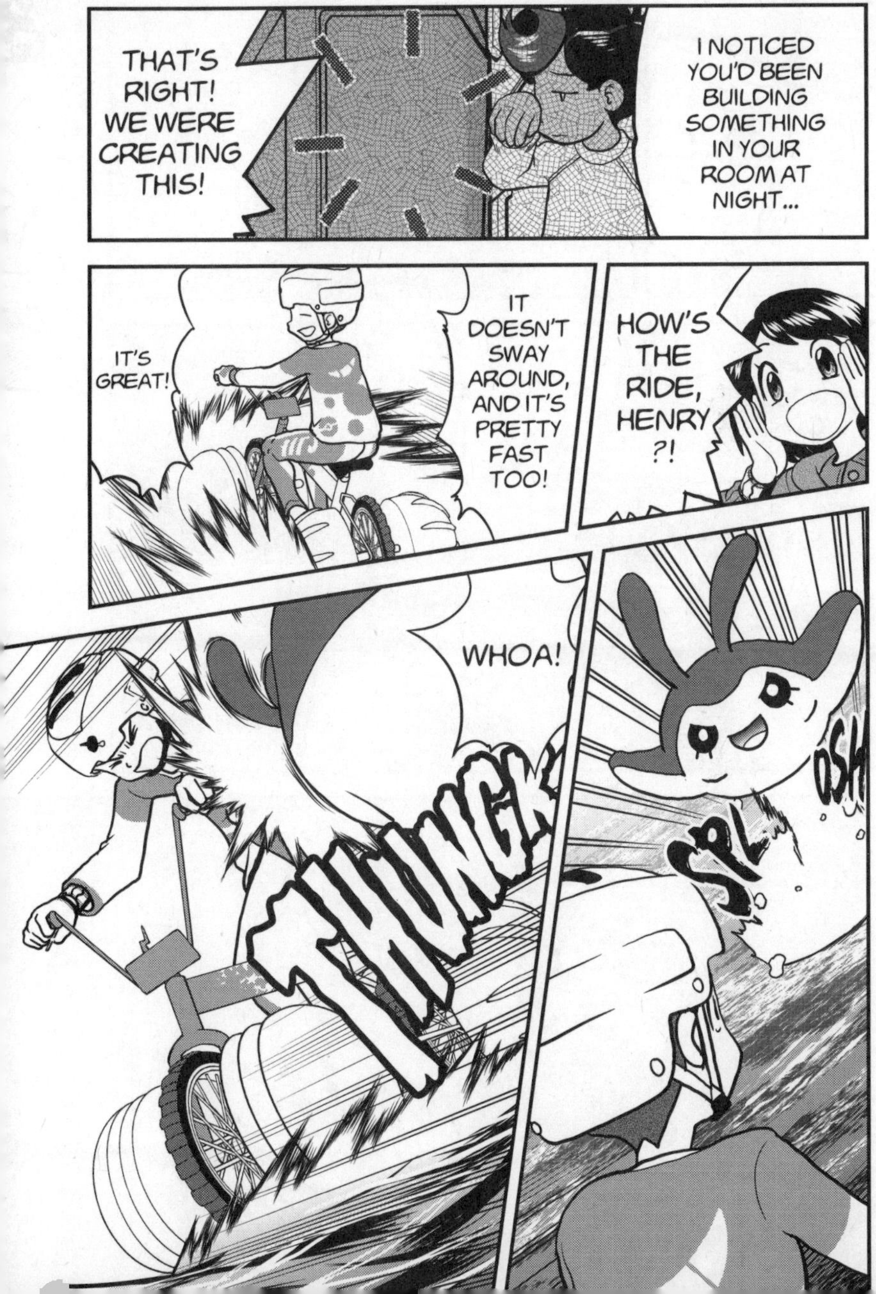
I NOTICED YOU'D BEEN BUILDING SOMETHING IN YOUR ROOM AT NIGHT...
THAT'S RIGHT! WE WERE CREATING THIS!
HOW'S THE RIDE, HENRY ?!
IT DOESN'T SWAY AROUND, AND IT'S PRETTY FAST TOO!
IT'S GREAT!
SPL
OSH
WHOA!
THUNGK!

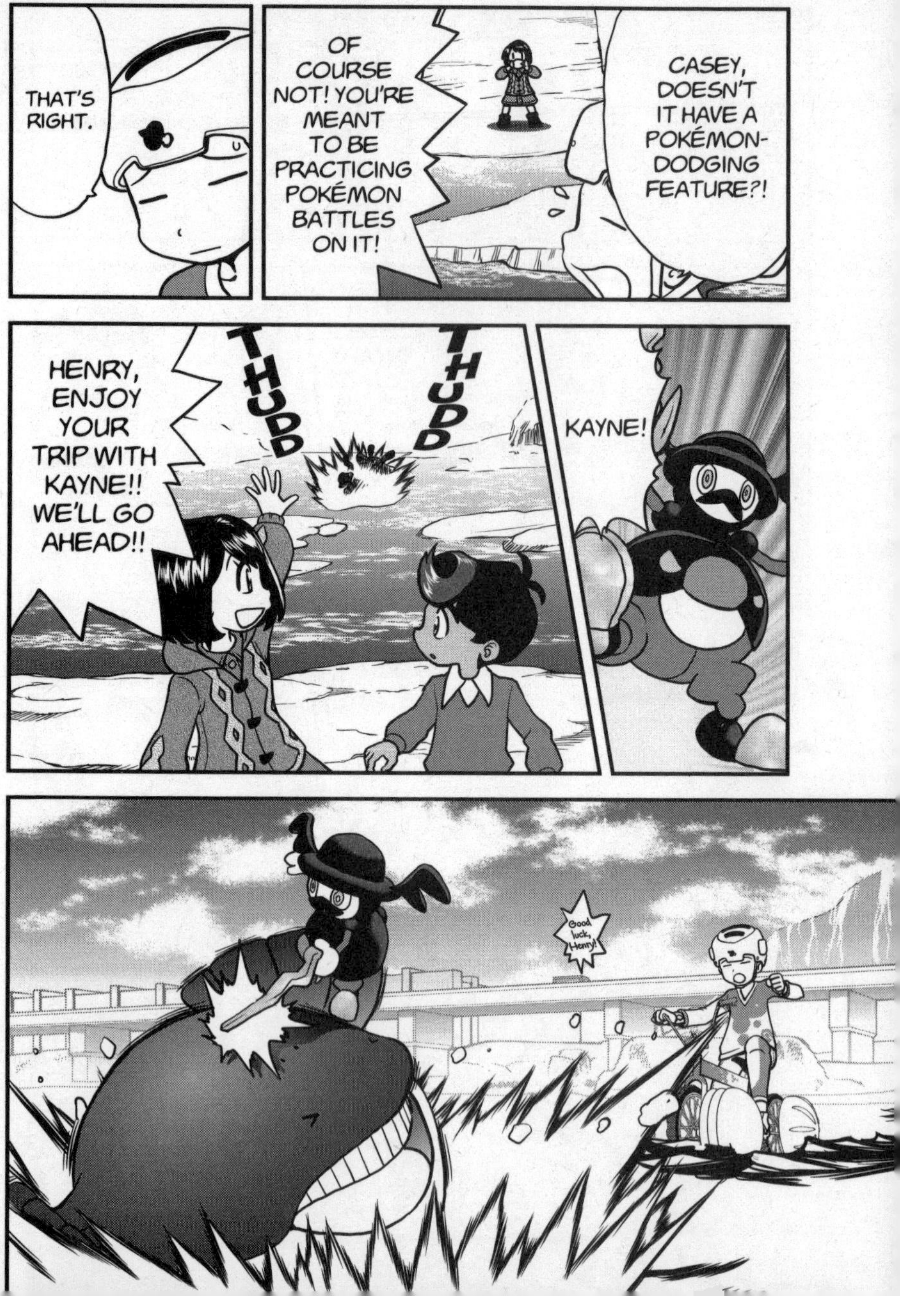
CASEY, DOESN'T IT HAVE A POKÉMON-DODGING FEATURE?!
OF COURSE NOT! YOU'RE MEANT TO BE PRACTICING POKÉMON BATTLES ON IT!
THAT'S RIGHT.
KAYNE!
THUDD
THUDD
HENRY, ENJOY YOUR TRIP WITH KAYNE!! WE'LL GO AHEAD!!
Good luck, Henry!

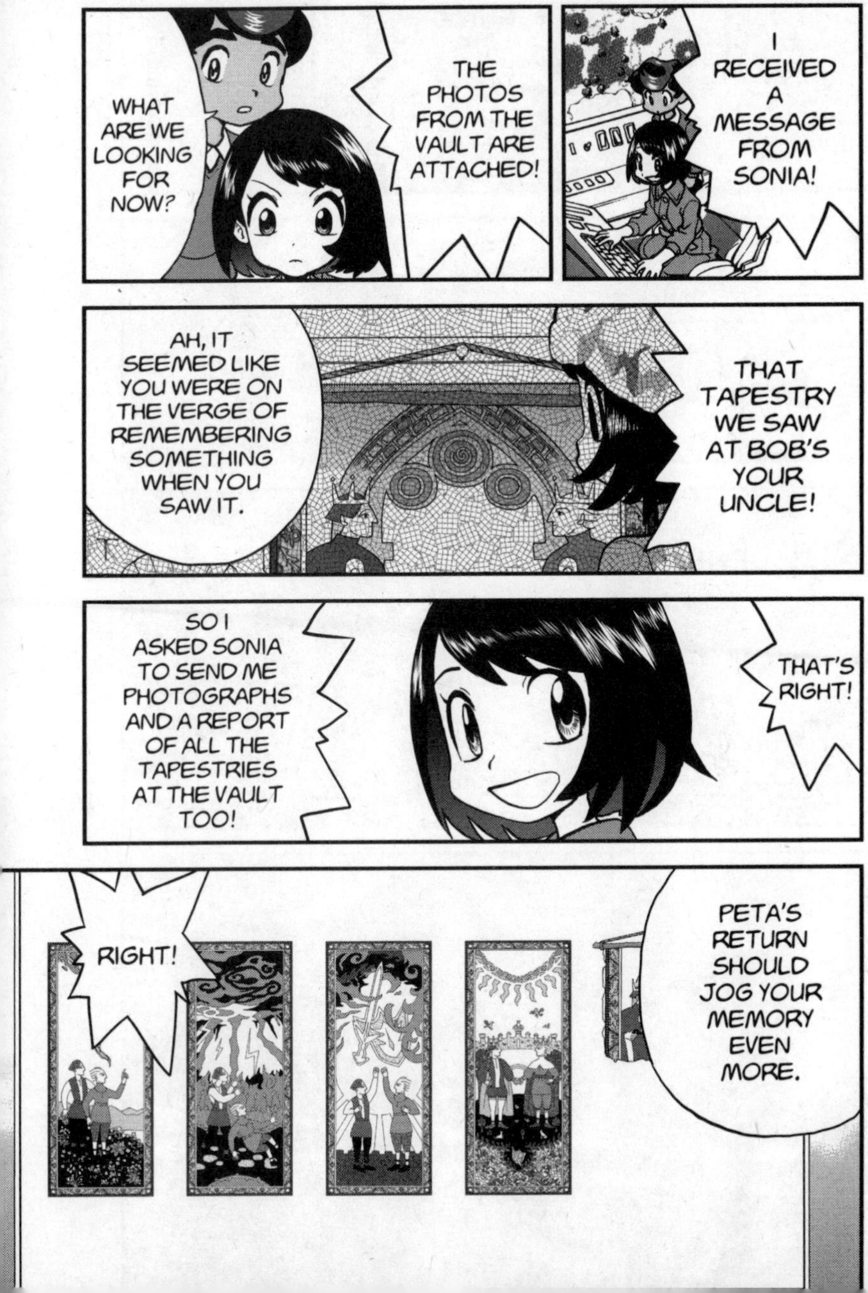
I RECEIVED A MESSAGE FROM SONIA!
THE PHOTOS FROM THE VAULT ARE ATTACHED!
WHAT ARE WE LOOKING FOR NOW?
THAT TAPESTRY WE SAW AT BOB'S YOUR UNCLE!
AH, IT SEEMED LIKE YOU WERE ON THE VERGE OF REMEMBERING SOMETHING WHEN YOU SAW IT.
THAT'S RIGHT!
SO I ASKED SONIA TO SEND ME PHOTOGRAPHS AND A REPORT OF ALL THE TAPESTRIES AT THE VAULT TOO!
PETA'S RETURN SHOULD JOG YOUR MEMORY EVEN MORE.
RIGHT!

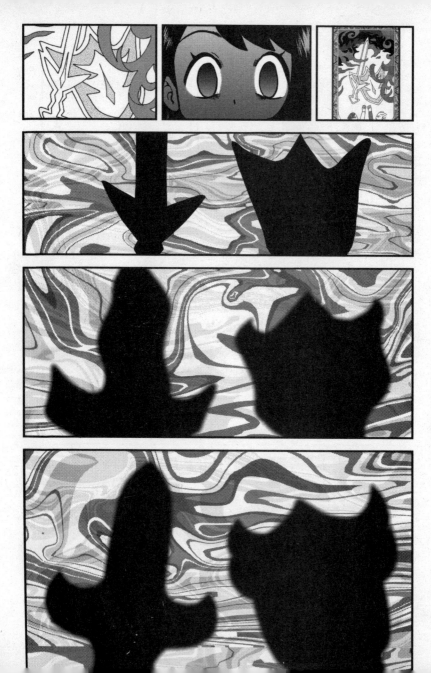

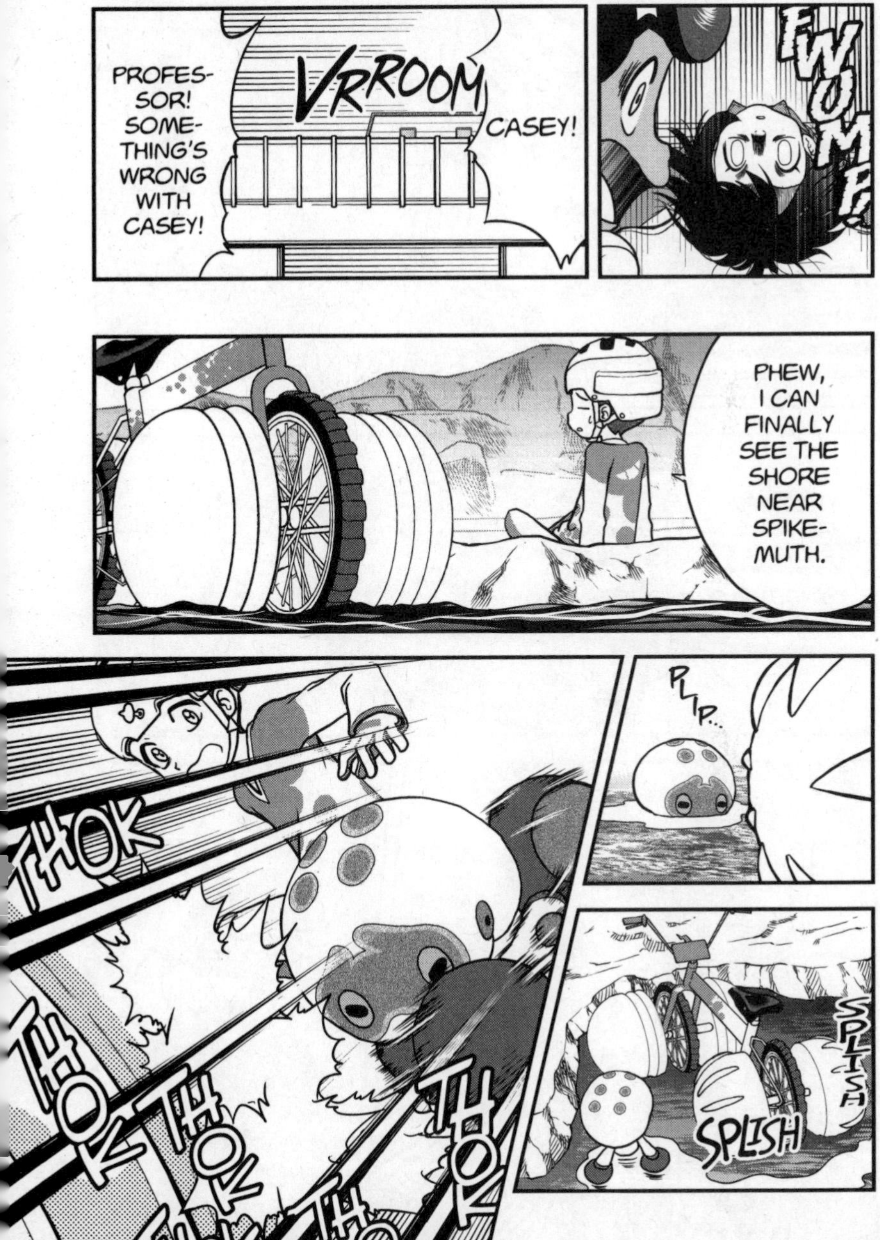
FWUMP!
VRROOM
CASEY!
PROFESSOR! SOMETHING'S WRONG WITH CASEY!
PHEW, I CAN FINALLY SEE THE SHORE NEAR SPIKEMUTH.
PLIP...
SPLISH
SPLISH
THOK
THOK
THOK
THOK
THOK
THOK

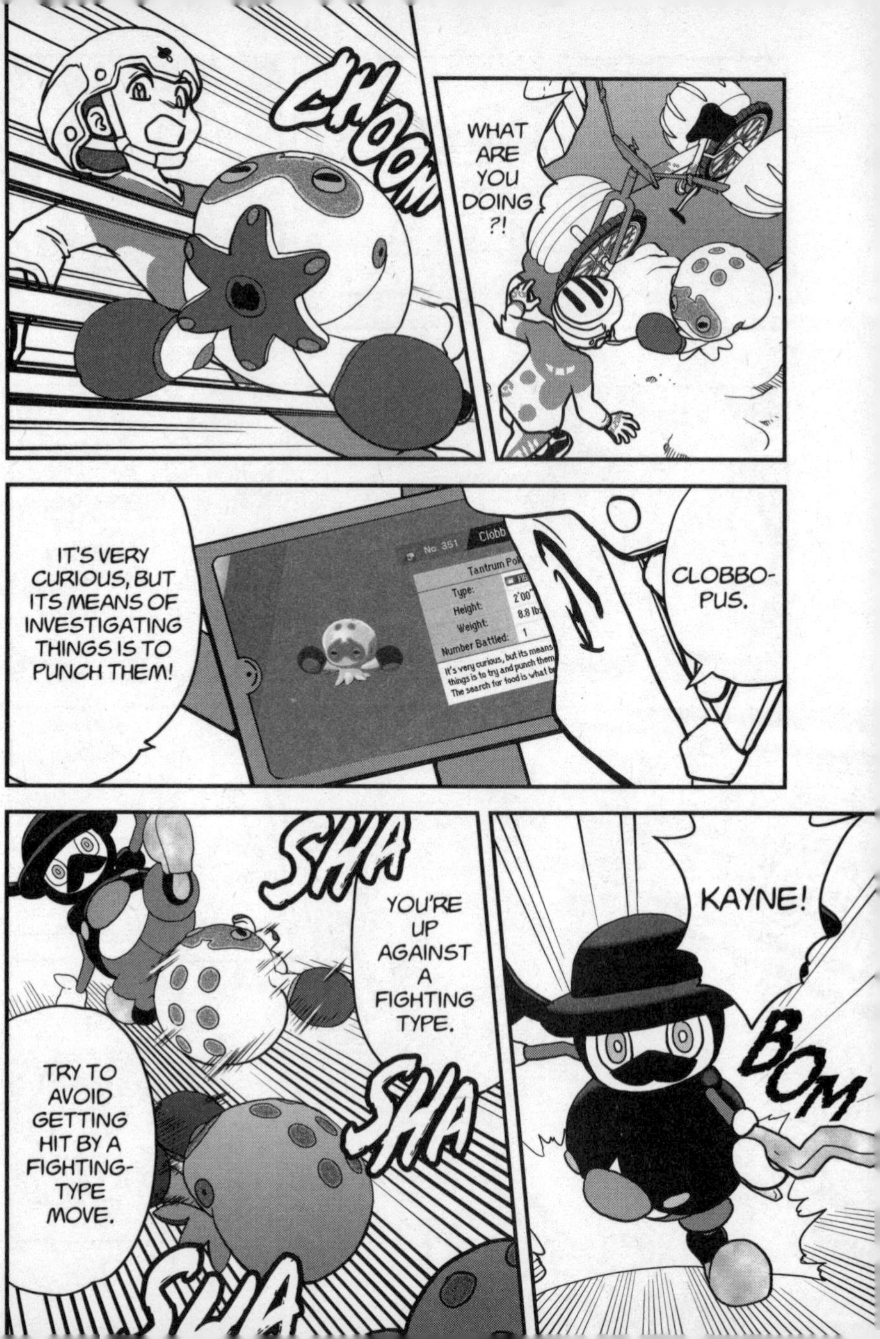
WHAT ARE YOU DOING ?!
CHOOON
CLOBBO-PUS.
No. 351
Type:
Height:
Weight:
Number Battled:
1
IT'S VERY CURIOUS, BUT ITS MEANS OF INVESTIGATING THINGS IS TO PUNCH THEM!
KAYNE!
BOM
SHA
YOU'RE UP AGAINST A FIGHTING TYPE.
TRY TO AVOID GETTING HIT BY A FIGHTING-TYPE MOVE.
SHA
SHA

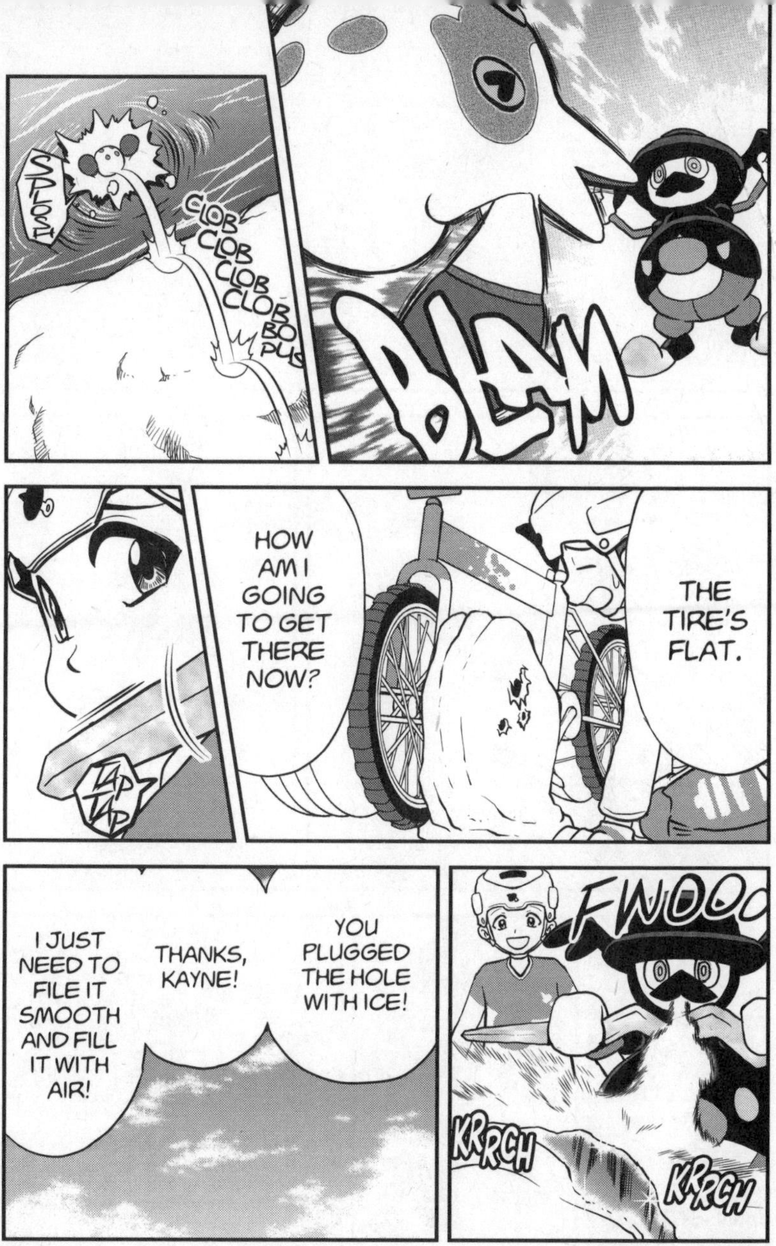
BLAM
SPLOSH
CLOB
CLOB
CLOB
CLOB
BO
PUS
THE TIRE'S FLAT.
HOW AM I GOING TO GET THERE NOW?
TAP TAP
FWOOO
KRRCH
KRRCH
YOU PLUGGED THE HOLE WITH ICE!
THANKS, KAYNE!
I JUST NEED TO FILE IT SMOOTH AND FILL IT WITH AIR!

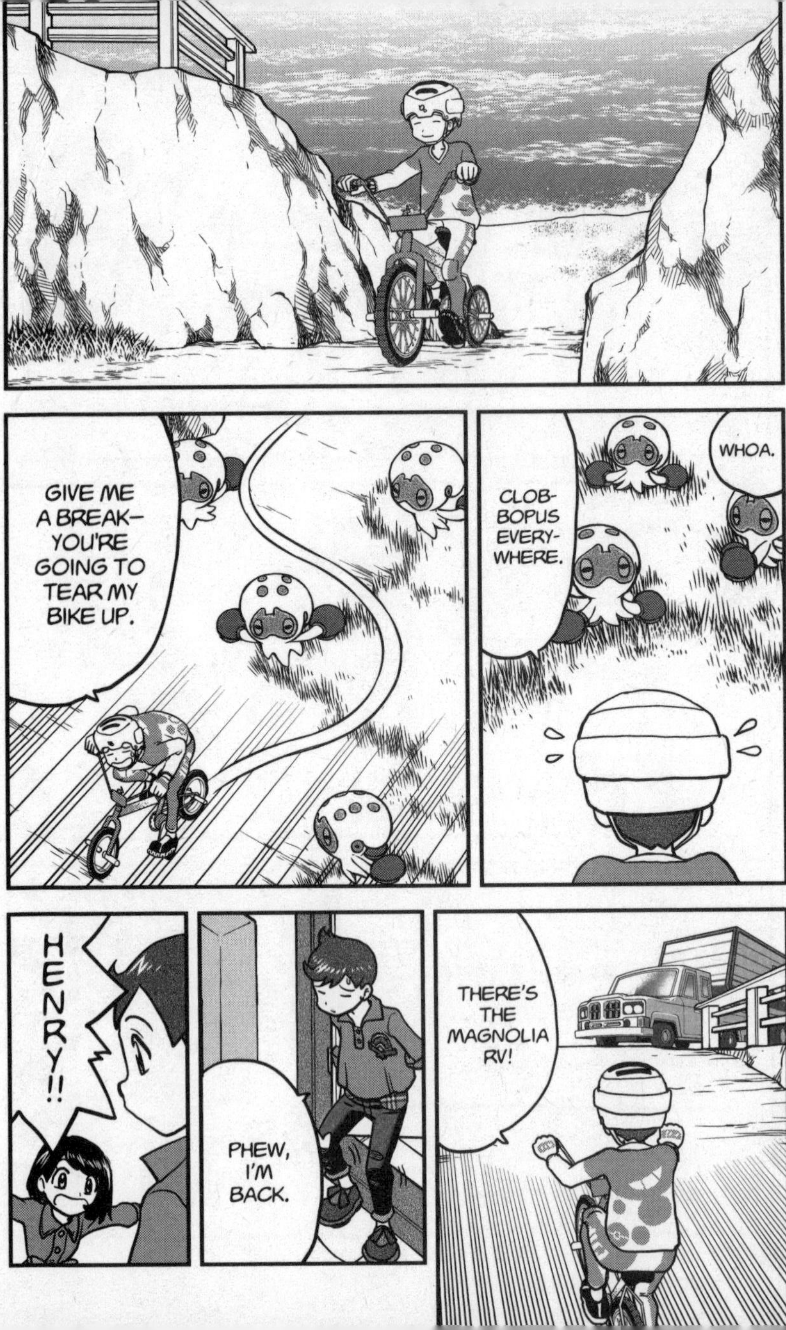
WHOA.
CLOB-BOPUS EVERY-WHERE.
GIVE ME A BREAK—YOU'RE GOING TO TEAR MY BIKE UP.
THERE'S THE MAGNOLIA RV!
PHEW, I'M BACK.
HENRY!!

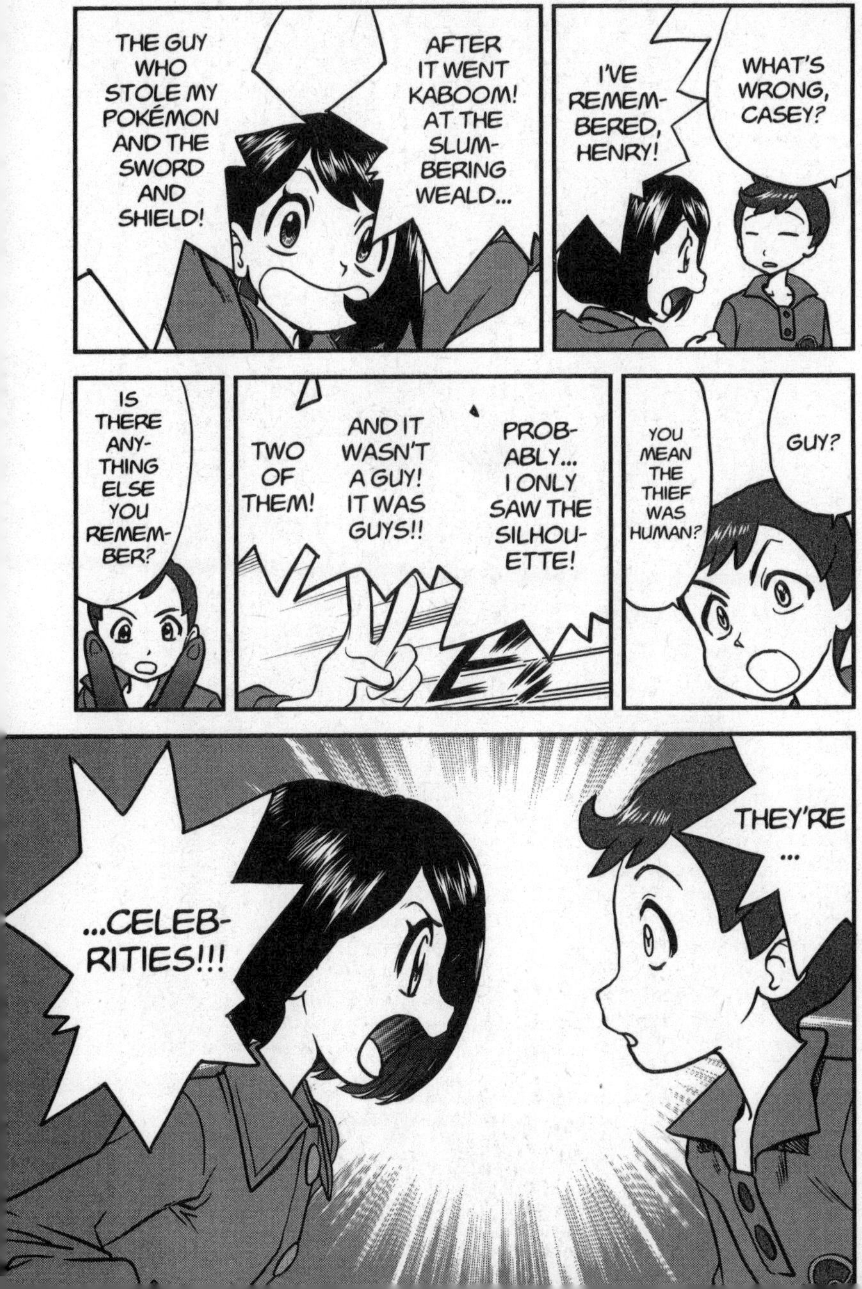
WHAT'S WRONG, CASEY?
I'VE REMEMBERED, HENRY!
AFTER IT WENT KABOOM! AT THE SLUMBERING WEALD...
THE GUY WHO STOLE MY POKÉMON AND THE SWORD AND SHIELD!
GUY?
YOU MEAN THE THIEF WAS HUMAN?
PROBABLY... I ONLY SAW THE SILHOUETTE!
AND IT WASN'T A GUY! IT WAS GUYS!!
TWO OF THEM!
IS THERE ANYTHING ELSE YOU REMEMBER?
THEY'RE ...
...CELEBRITIES!!!

GIGANTAMAX DREDNAW

TYPE:	Water, Rock
ABILITY:	Strong Jaw Shell Armor
G-MAX MOVE:	G-Max Stonesurge

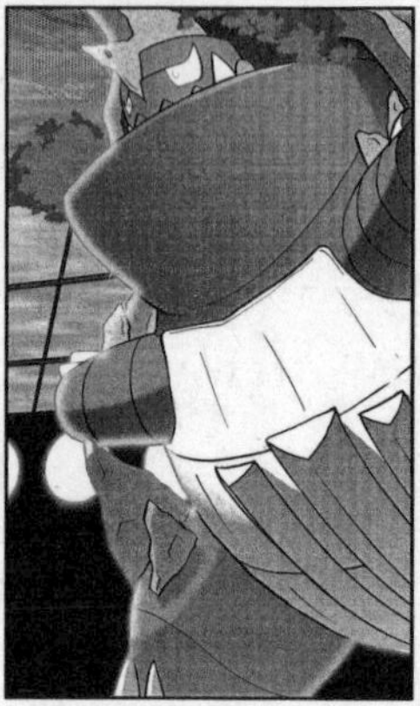

HEIGHT:	78'9"+
WEIGHT:	??? lbs

ORDINARY

DREDNAW

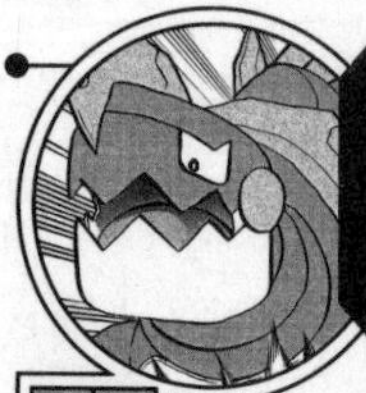

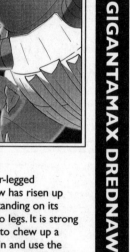

HEIGHT:	3'3"
WEIGHT:	254.6 lbs

The four-legged Drednaw has risen up and is standing on its back two legs. It is strong enough to chew up a mountain and use the rubble to stop a flood. In a battle, it will crush its opponent and bite the opponent with its powerful jaw!

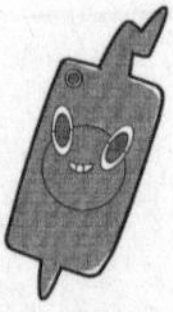

STRATEGY NOTES

The Water-type move used by Gigantamax Drednaw is G-Max Stonesurge. The move spreads sharp rocks everywhere to inflict damage. Be extra careful when switching your Pokémon out, as that decision could determine the course of battle.

Adventure 22 Grrr!! Noble Kidnappers

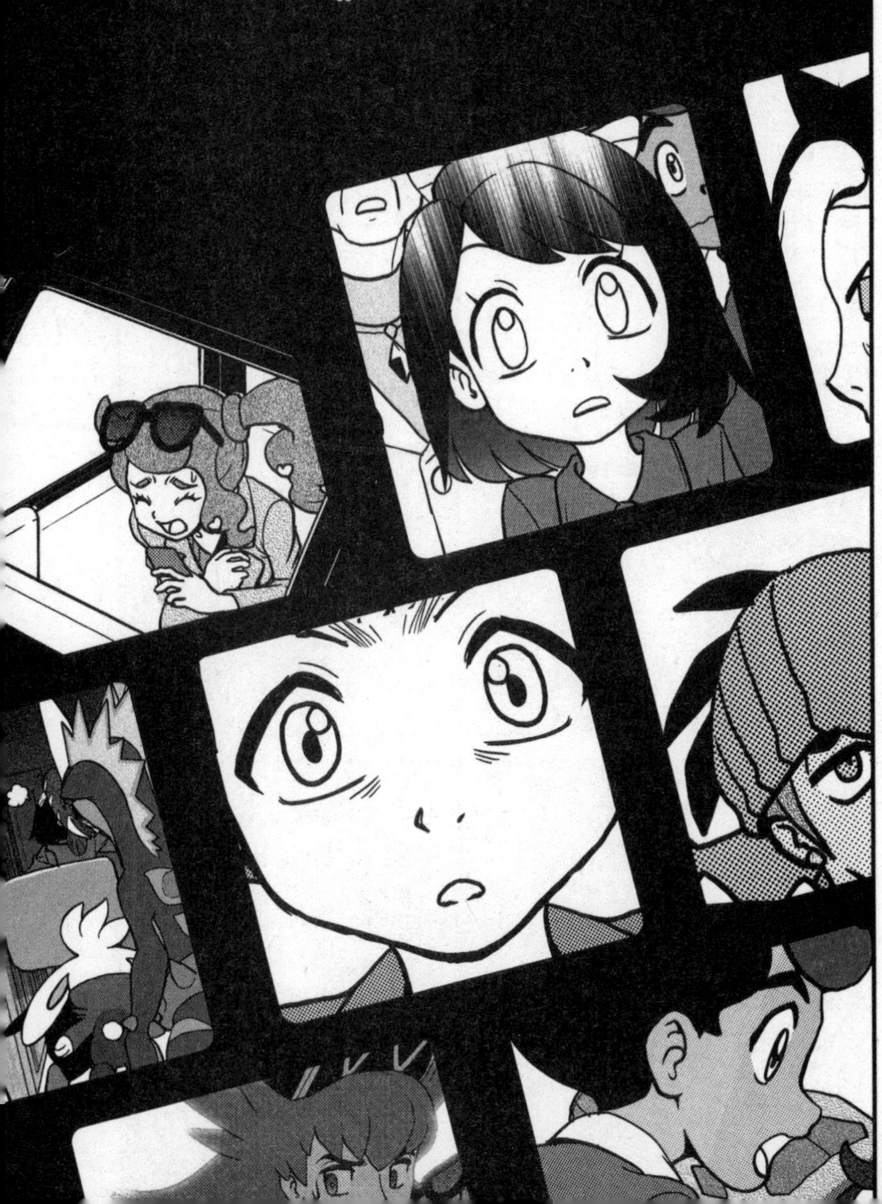

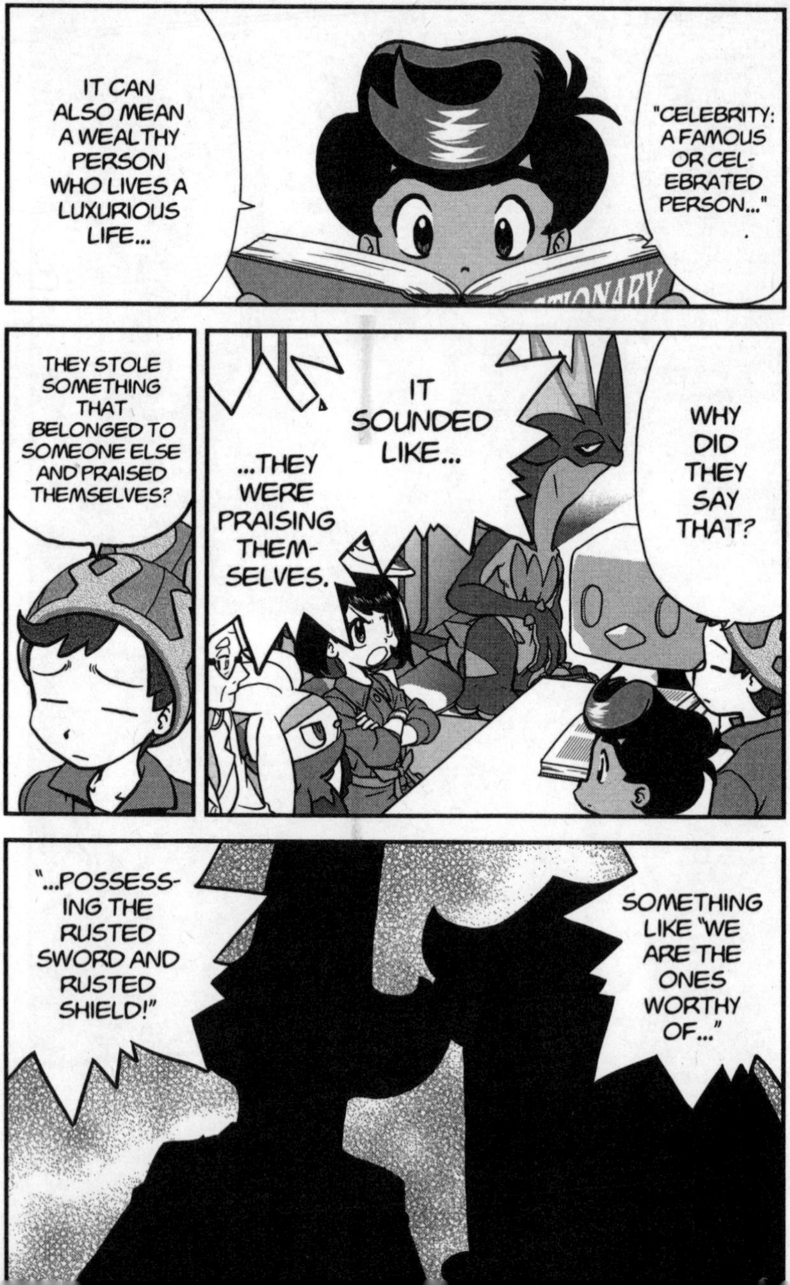
"CELEBRITY: A FAMOUS OR CELEBRATED PERSON..."
IT CAN ALSO MEAN A WEALTHY PERSON WHO LIVES A LUXURIOUS LIFE...
WHY DID THEY SAY THAT?
IT SOUNDED LIKE...
...THEY WERE PRAISING THEMSELVES.
THEY STOLE SOMETHING THAT BELONGED TO SOMEONE ELSE AND PRAISED THEMSELVES?
SOMETHING LIKE "WE ARE THE ONES WORTHY OF..."
"...POSSESSING THE RUSTED SWORD AND RUSTED SHIELD!"

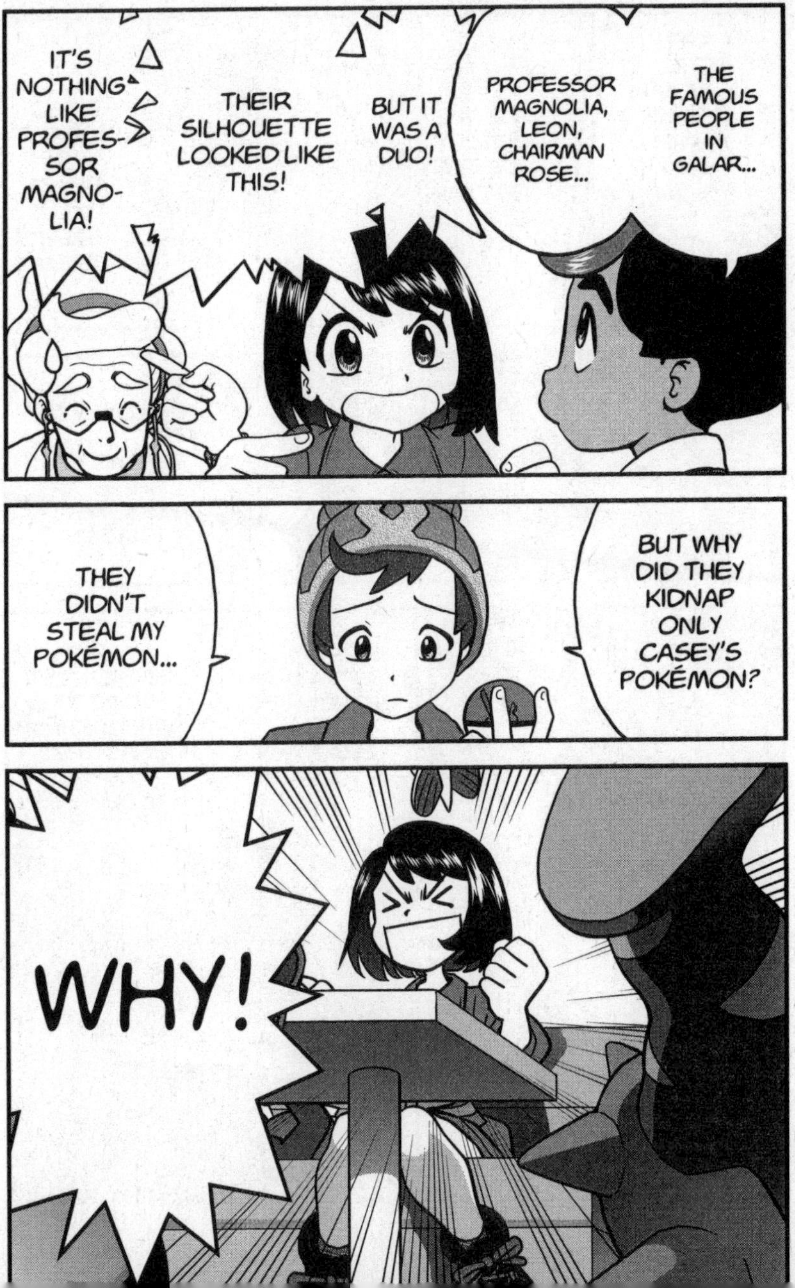
THE FAMOUS PEOPLE IN GALAR...
PROFESSOR MAGNOLIA, LEON, CHAIRMAN ROSE...
BUT IT WAS A DUO!
THEIR SILHOUETTE LOOKED LIKE THIS!
IT'S NOTHING LIKE PROFES-SOR MAGNO-LIA!
BUT WHY DID THEY KIDNAP ONLY CASEY'S POKÉMON?
THEY DIDN'T STEAL MY POKÉMON...
WHY!

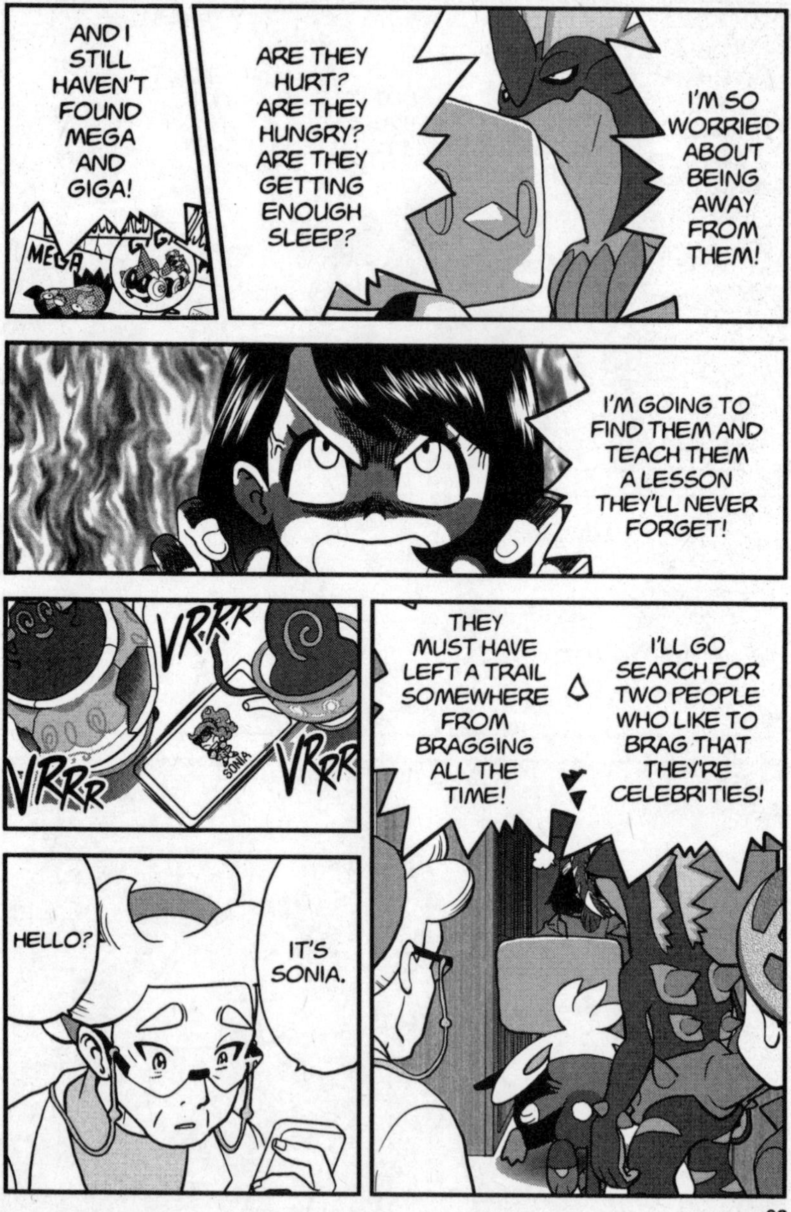
I'M SO WORRIED ABOUT BEING AWAY FROM THEM!
ARE THEY HURT? ARE THEY HUNGRY? ARE THEY GETTING ENOUGH SLEEP?
AND I STILL HAVEN'T FOUND MEGA AND GIGA!
I'M GOING TO FIND THEM AND TEACH THEM A LESSON THEY'LL NEVER FORGET!
I'LL GO SEARCH FOR TWO PEOPLE WHO LIKE TO BRAG THAT THEY'RE CELEBRITIES!
THEY MUST HAVE LEFT A TRAIL SOMEWHERE FROM BRAGGING ALL THE TIME!
VRRR
SONIA
VRRR
IT'S SONIA.
HELLO?

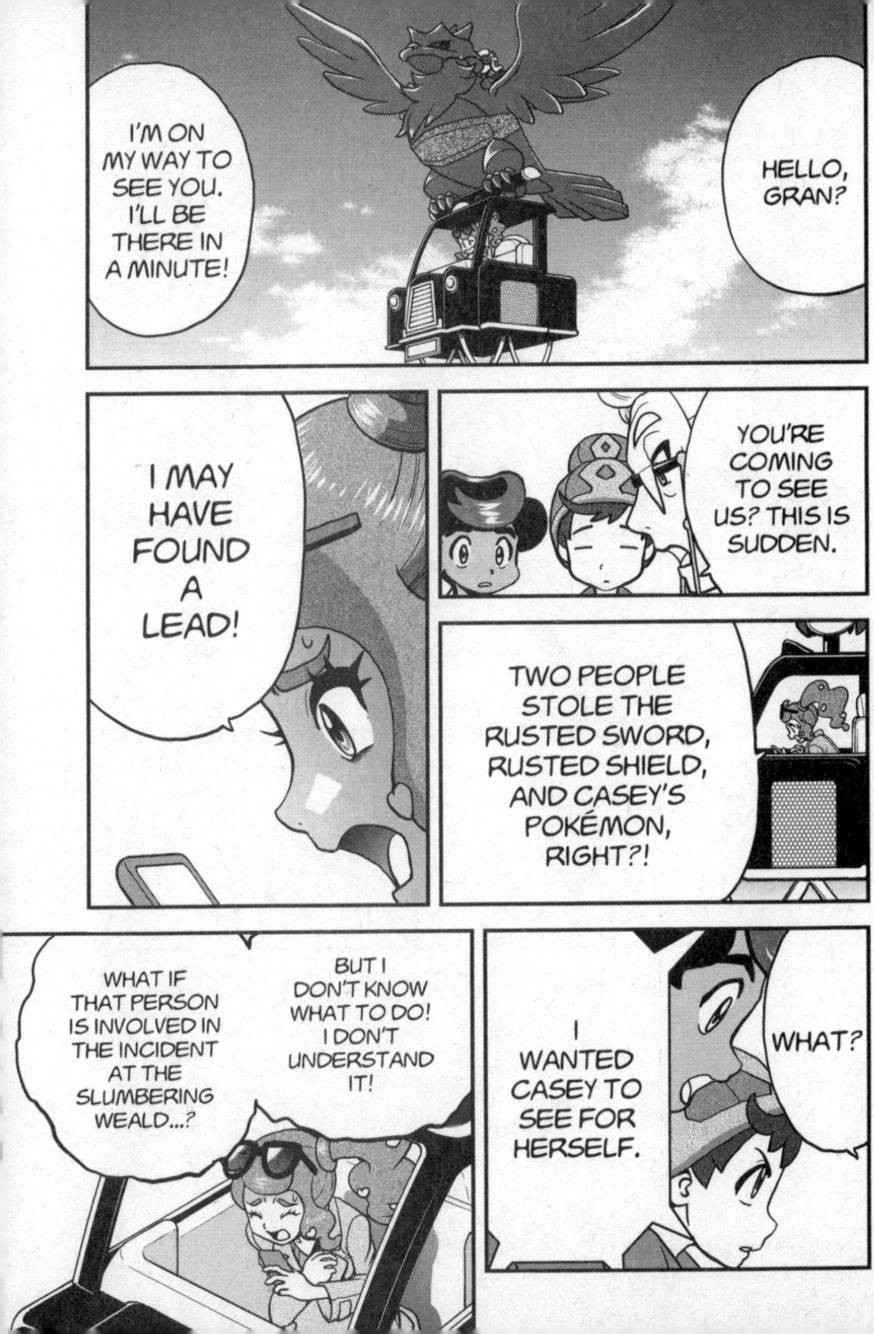
HELLO, GRAN?
I'M ON MY WAY TO SEE YOU. I'LL BE THERE IN A MINUTE!
YOU'RE COMING TO SEE US? THIS IS SUDDEN.
TWO PEOPLE STOLE THE RUSTED SWORD, RUSTED SHIELD, AND CASEY'S POKÉMON, RIGHT?!
I MAY HAVE FOUND A LEAD!
WHAT?
I WANTED CASEY TO SEE FOR HERSELF.
BUT I DON'T KNOW WHAT TO DO! I DON'T UNDERSTAND IT!
WHAT IF THAT PERSON IS INVOLVED IN THE INCIDENT AT THE SLUMBERING WEALD...?

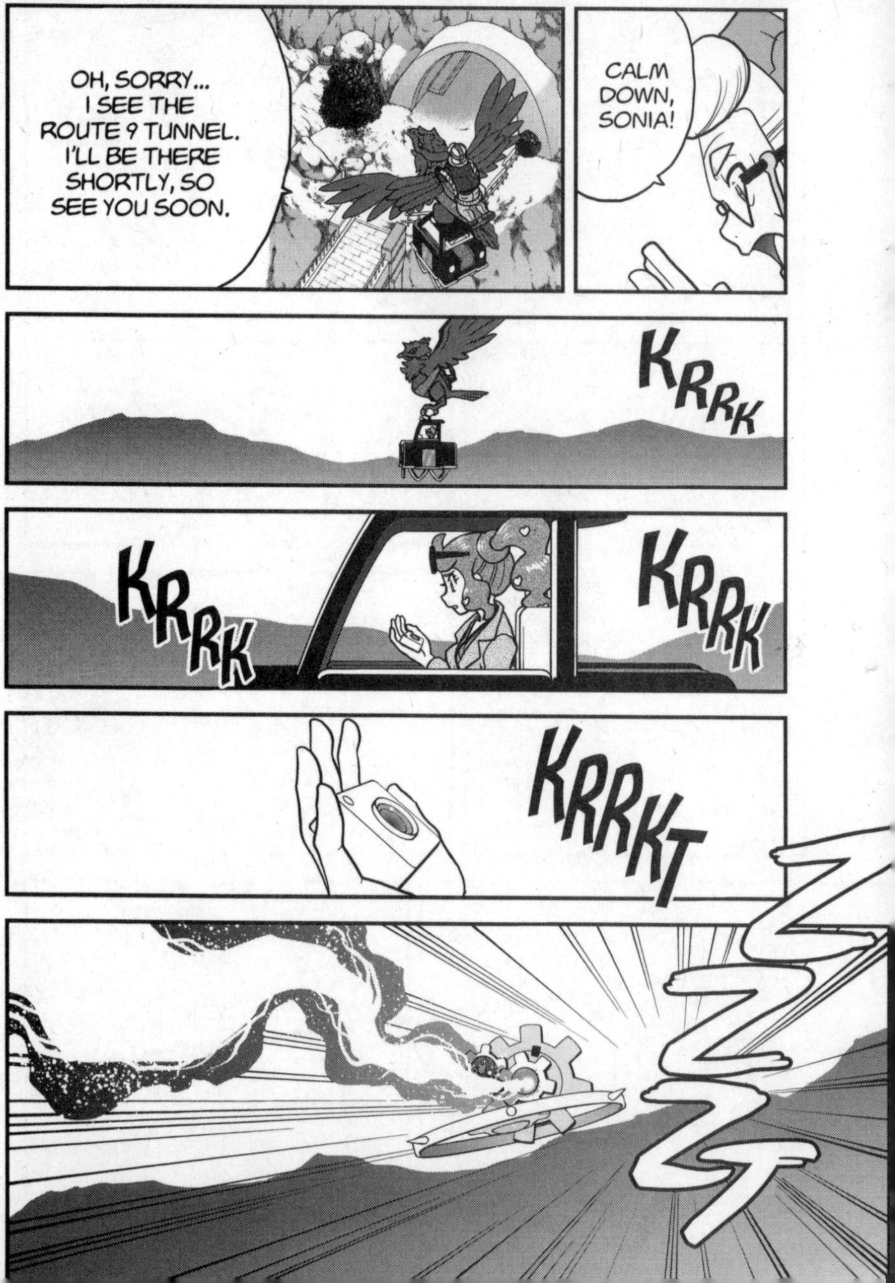
CALM DOWN, SONIA!
OH, SORRY... I SEE THE ROUTE 9 TUNNEL. I'LL BE THERE SHORTLY, SO SEE YOU SOON.
KRRRK
KRRRK
KRRRK
KRRRKT
ZZZT

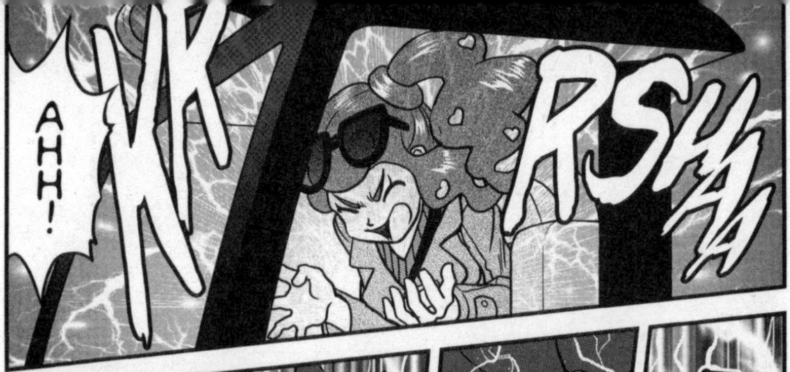
RSHAA
KK
AHH!
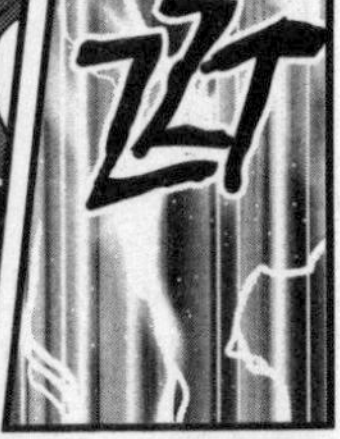
ZZT
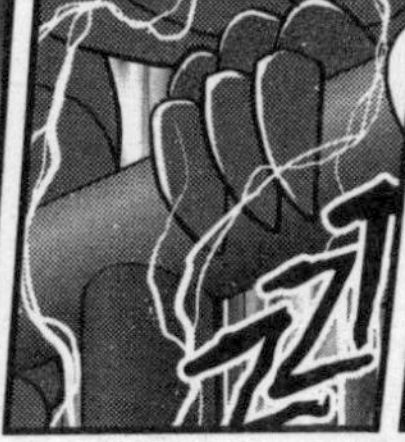
ZZT
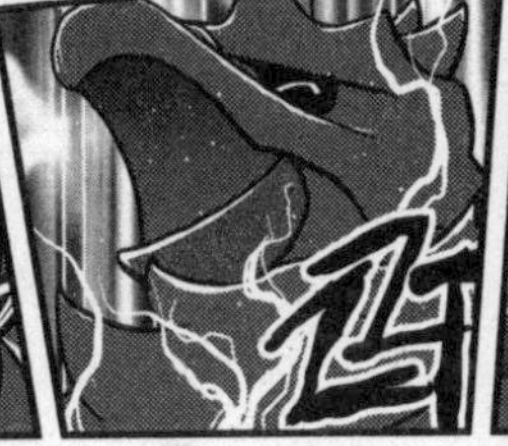
ZZT
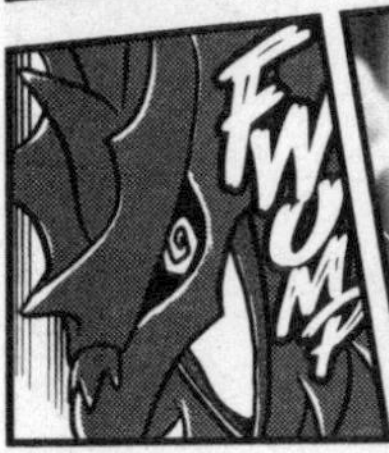
FWUMP
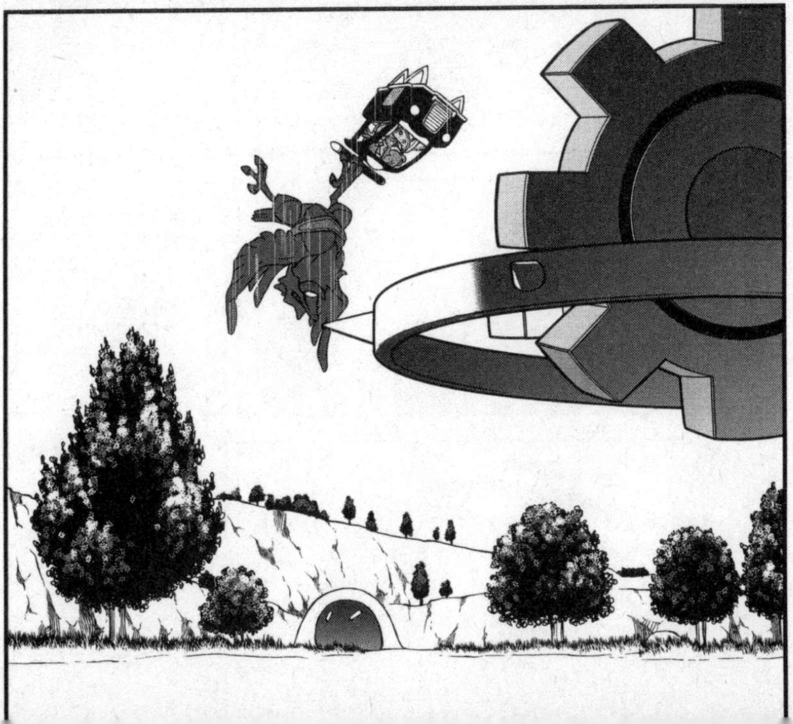

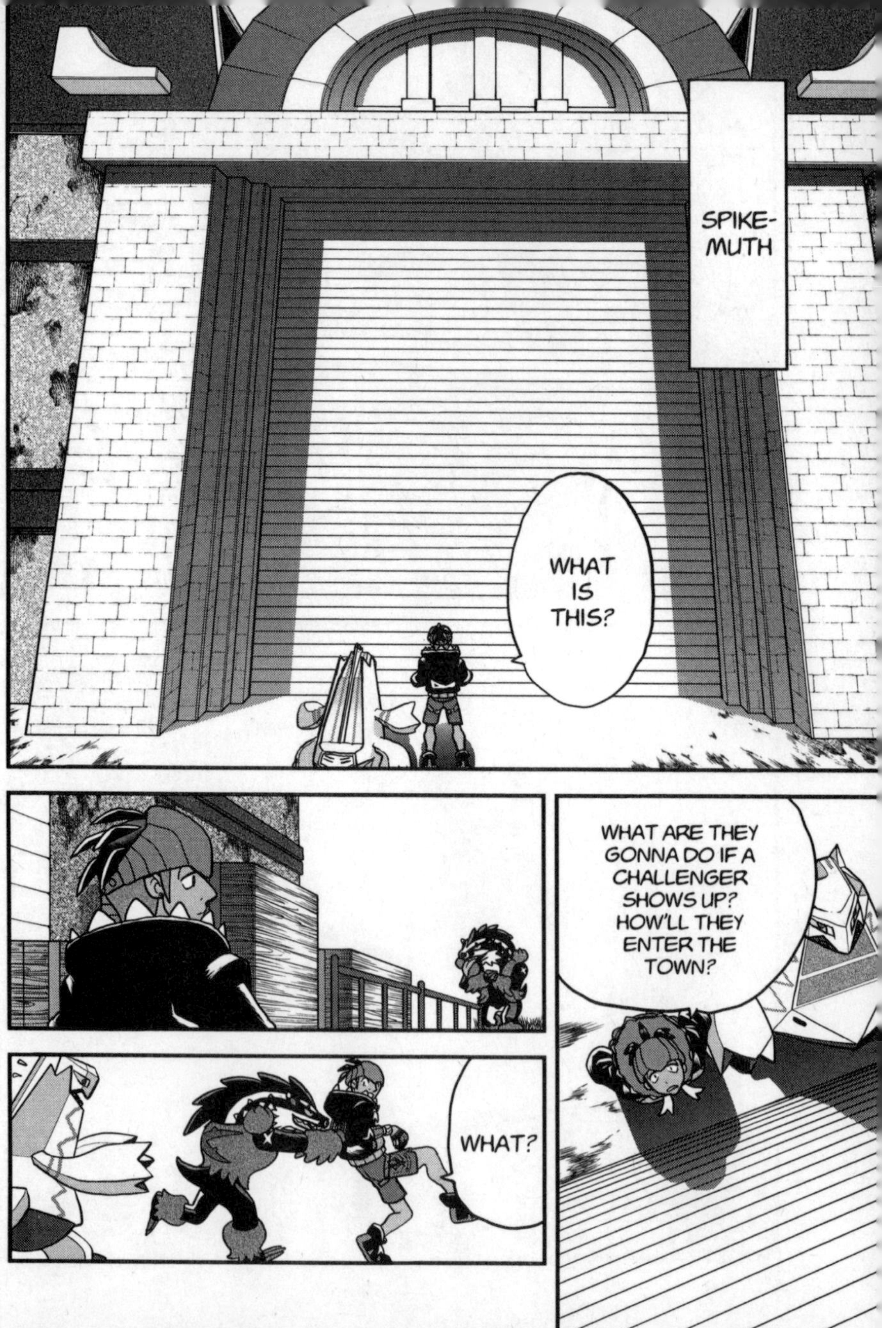
SPIKE-
MUTH
WHAT IS THIS?
WHAT ARE THEY GONNA DO IF A CHALLENGER SHOWS UP? HOW'LL THEY ENTER THE TOWN?
WHAT?

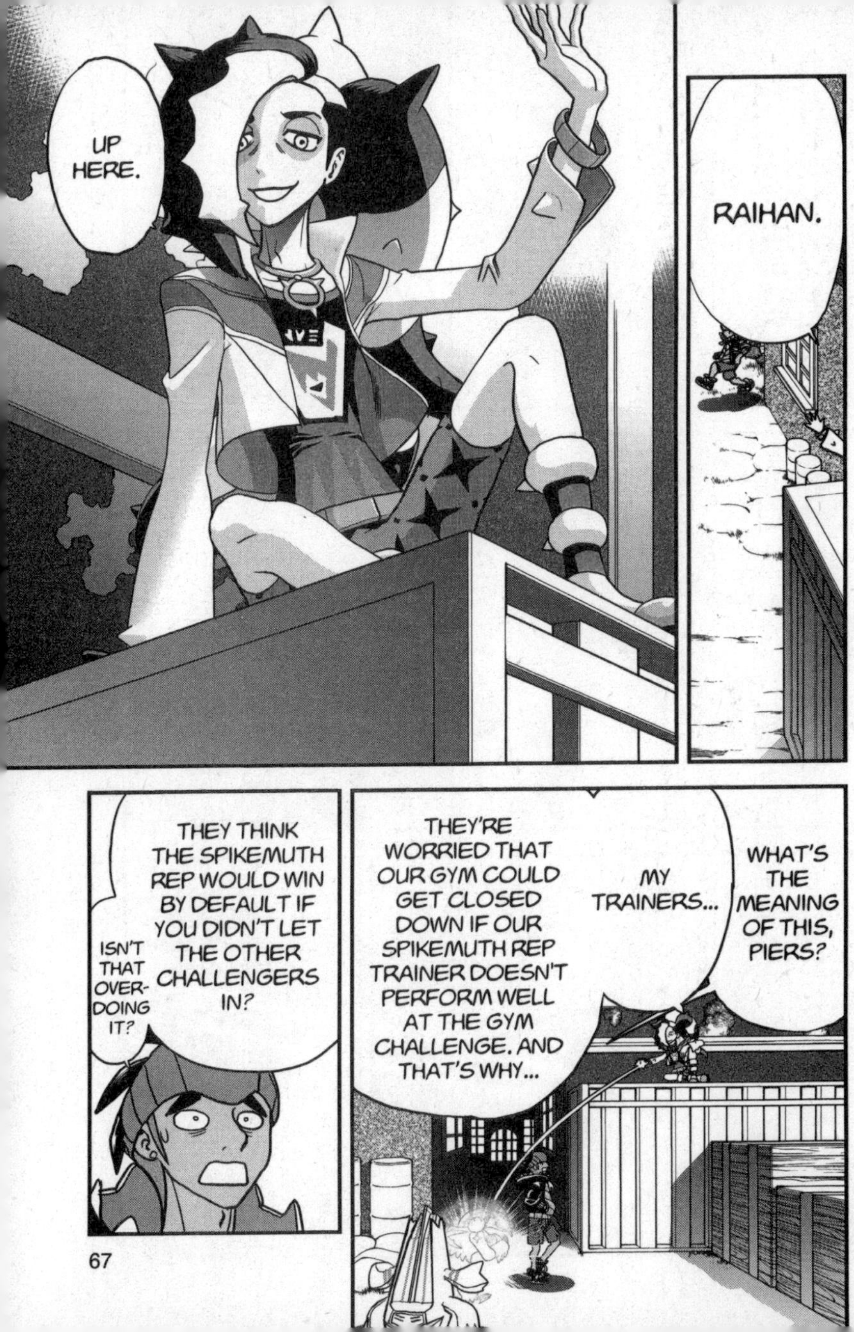
RAIHAN.
UP HERE.
WHAT'S THE MEANING OF THIS, PIERS?
MY TRAINERS...
THEY'RE WORRIED THAT OUR GYM COULD GET CLOSED DOWN IF OUR SPIKEMUTH REP TRAINER DOESN'T PERFORM WELL AT THE GYM CHALLENGE. AND THAT'S WHY...
THEY THINK THE SPIKEMUTH REP WOULD WIN BY DEFAULT IF YOU DIDN'T LET THE OTHER CHALLENGERS IN?
ISN'T THAT OVER-DOING IT?

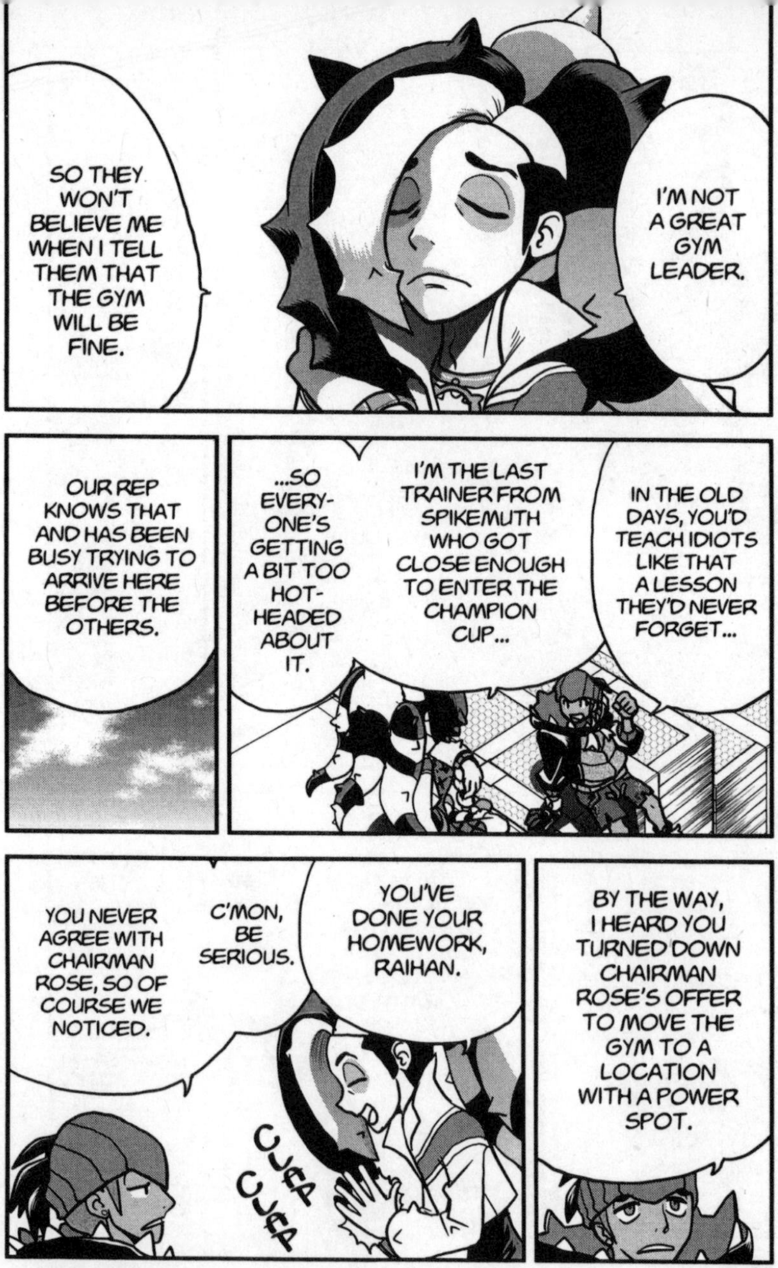
I'M NOT A GREAT GYM LEADER.
SO THEY WON'T BELIEVE ME WHEN I TELL THEM THAT THE GYM WILL BE FINE.
IN THE OLD DAYS, YOU'D TEACH IDIOTS LIKE THAT A LESSON THEY'D NEVER FORGET...
I'M THE LAST TRAINER FROM SPIKEMUTH WHO GOT CLOSE ENOUGH TO ENTER THE CHAMPION CUP...
...SO EVERY-ONE'S GETTING A BIT TOO HOT-HEADED ABOUT IT.
OUR REP KNOWS THAT AND HAS BEEN BUSY TRYING TO ARRIVE HERE BEFORE THE OTHERS.
BY THE WAY, I HEARD YOU TURNED DOWN CHAIRMAN ROSE'S OFFER TO MOVE THE GYM TO A LOCATION WITH A POWER SPOT.
YOU'VE DONE YOUR HOMEWORK, RAIHAN.
C'MON, BE SERIOUS.
YOU NEVER AGREE WITH CHAIRMAN ROSE, SO OF COURSE WE NOTICED.
CLAP CLAP

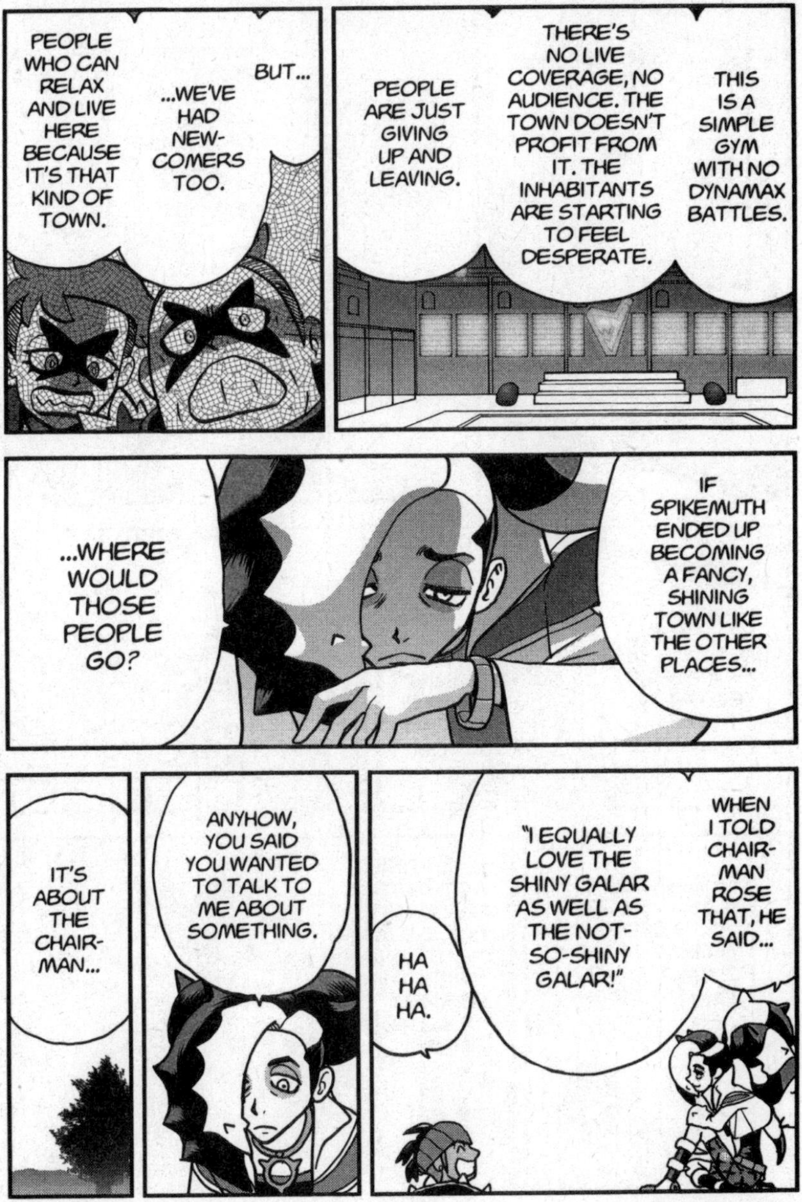
THIS IS A SIMPLE GYM WITH NO DYNAMAX BATTLES.
THERE'S NO LIVE COVERAGE, NO AUDIENCE. THE TOWN DOESN'T PROFIT FROM IT. THE INHABITANTS ARE STARTING TO FEEL DESPERATE.
PEOPLE ARE JUST GIVING UP AND LEAVING.
BUT...
...WE'VE HAD NEW-COMERS TOO.
PEOPLE WHO CAN RELAX AND LIVE HERE BECAUSE IT'S THAT KIND OF TOWN.
IF SPIKEMUTH ENDED UP BECOMING A FANCY, SHINING TOWN LIKE THE OTHER PLACES...
...WHERE WOULD THOSE PEOPLE GO?
WHEN I TOLD CHAIR-MAN ROSE THAT, HE SAID...
"I EQUALLY LOVE THE SHINY GALAR AS WELL AS THE NOT-SO-SHINY GALAR!"
HA HA HA.
ANYHOW, YOU SAID YOU WANTED TO TALK TO ME ABOUT SOMETHING.
IT'S ABOUT THE CHAIR-MAN...

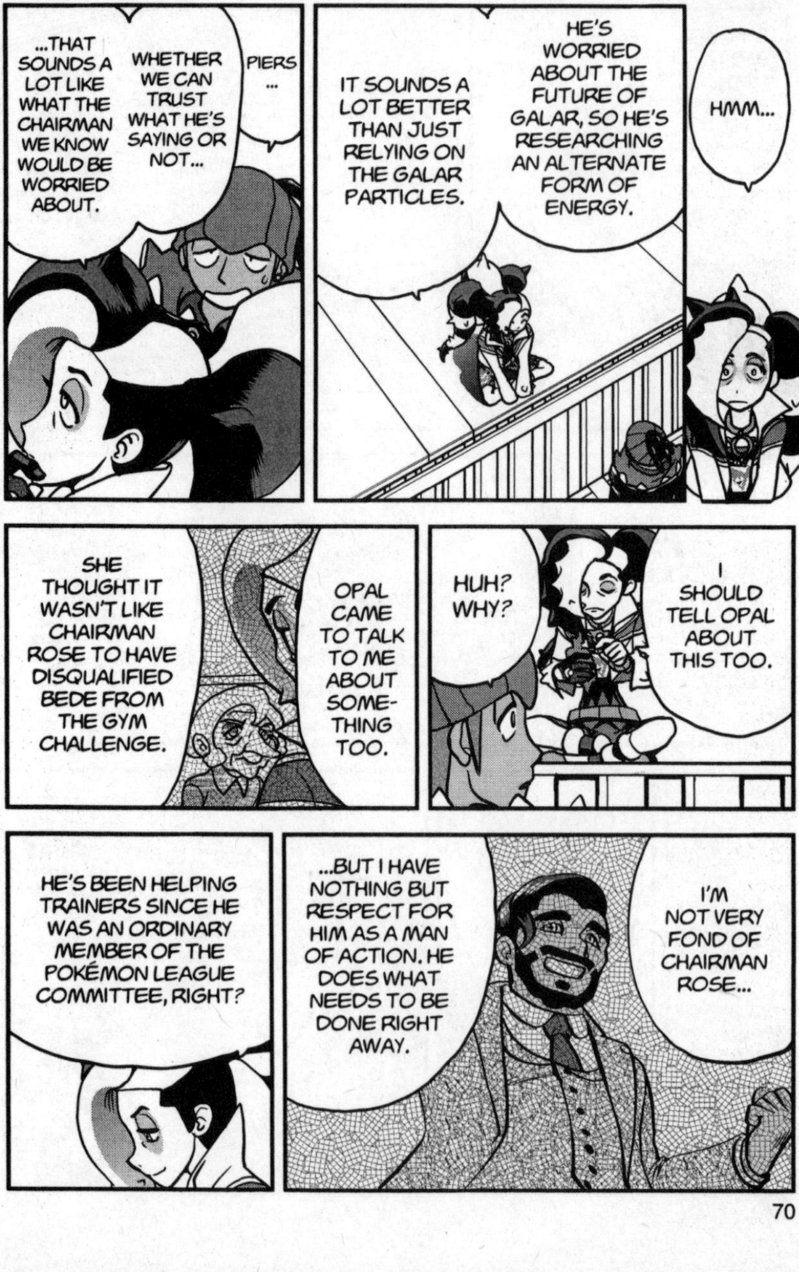
HMM...
HE'S WORRIED ABOUT THE FUTURE OF GALAR, SO HE'S RESEARCHING AN ALTERNATE FORM OF ENERGY.
IT SOUNDS A LOT BETTER THAN JUST RELYING ON THE GALAR PARTICLES.
PIERS ...
WHETHER WE CAN TRUST WHAT HE'S SAYING OR NOT...
...THAT SOUNDS A LOT LIKE WHAT THE CHAIRMAN WE KNOW WOULD BE WORRIED ABOUT.
I SHOULD TELL OPAL ABOUT THIS TOO.
HUH? WHY?
OPAL CAME TO TALK TO ME ABOUT SOME-THING TOO.
SHE THOUGHT IT WASN'T LIKE CHAIRMAN ROSE TO HAVE DISQUALIFIED BEDE FROM THE GYM CHALLENGE.
I'M NOT VERY FOND OF CHAIRMAN ROSE...
...BUT I HAVE NOTHING BUT RESPECT FOR HIM AS A MAN OF ACTION. HE DOES WHAT NEEDS TO BE DONE RIGHT AWAY.
HE'S BEEN HELPING TRAINERS SINCE HE WAS AN ORDINARY MEMBER OF THE POKÉMON LEAGUE COMMITTEE, RIGHT?

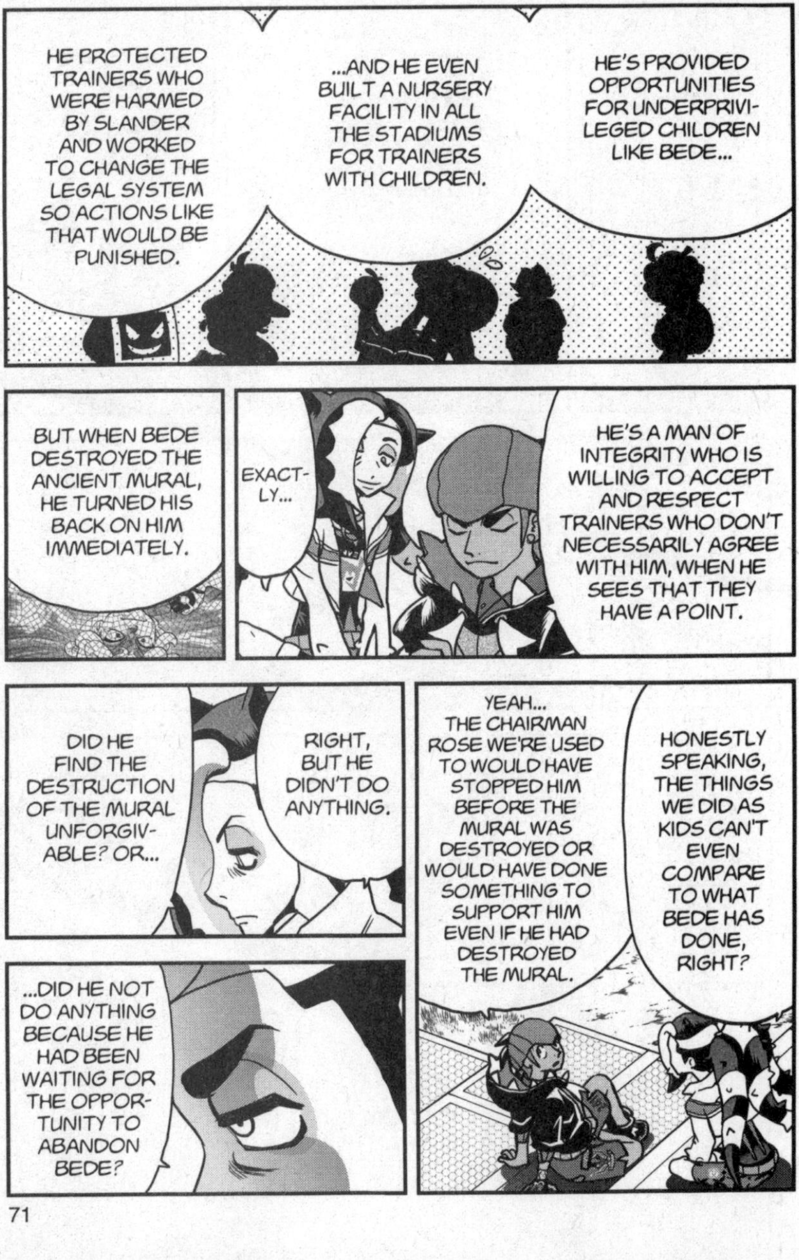
HE'S PROVIDED OPPORTUNITIES FOR UNDERPRIVI-LEGED CHILDREN LIKE BEDE...
...AND HE EVEN BUILT A NURSERY FACILITY IN ALL THE STADIUMS FOR TRAINERS WITH CHILDREN.
HE PROTECTED TRAINERS WHO WERE HARMED BY SLANDER AND WORKED TO CHANGE THE LEGAL SYSTEM SO ACTIONS LIKE THAT WOULD BE PUNISHED.
HE'S A MAN OF INTEGRITY WHO IS WILLING TO ACCEPT AND RESPECT TRAINERS WHO DON'T NECESSARILY AGREE WITH HIM, WHEN HE SEES THAT THEY HAVE A POINT.
EXACT-LY...
BUT WHEN BEDE DESTROYED THE ANCIENT MURAL, HE TURNED HIS BACK ON HIM IMMEDIATELY.
HONESTLY SPEAKING, THE THINGS WE DID AS KIDS CAN'T EVEN COMPARE TO WHAT BEDE HAS DONE, RIGHT?
YEAH... THE CHAIRMAN ROSE WE'RE USED TO WOULD HAVE STOPPED HIM BEFORE THE MURAL WAS DESTROYED OR WOULD HAVE DONE SOMETHING TO SUPPORT HIM EVEN IF HE HAD DESTROYED THE MURAL.
RIGHT, BUT HE DIDN'T DO ANYTHING.
DID HE FIND THE DESTRUCTION OF THE MURAL UNFORGIV-ABLE? OR...
...DID HE NOT DO ANYTHING BECAUSE HE HAD BEEN WAITING FOR THE OPPOR-TUNITY TO ABANDON BEDE?

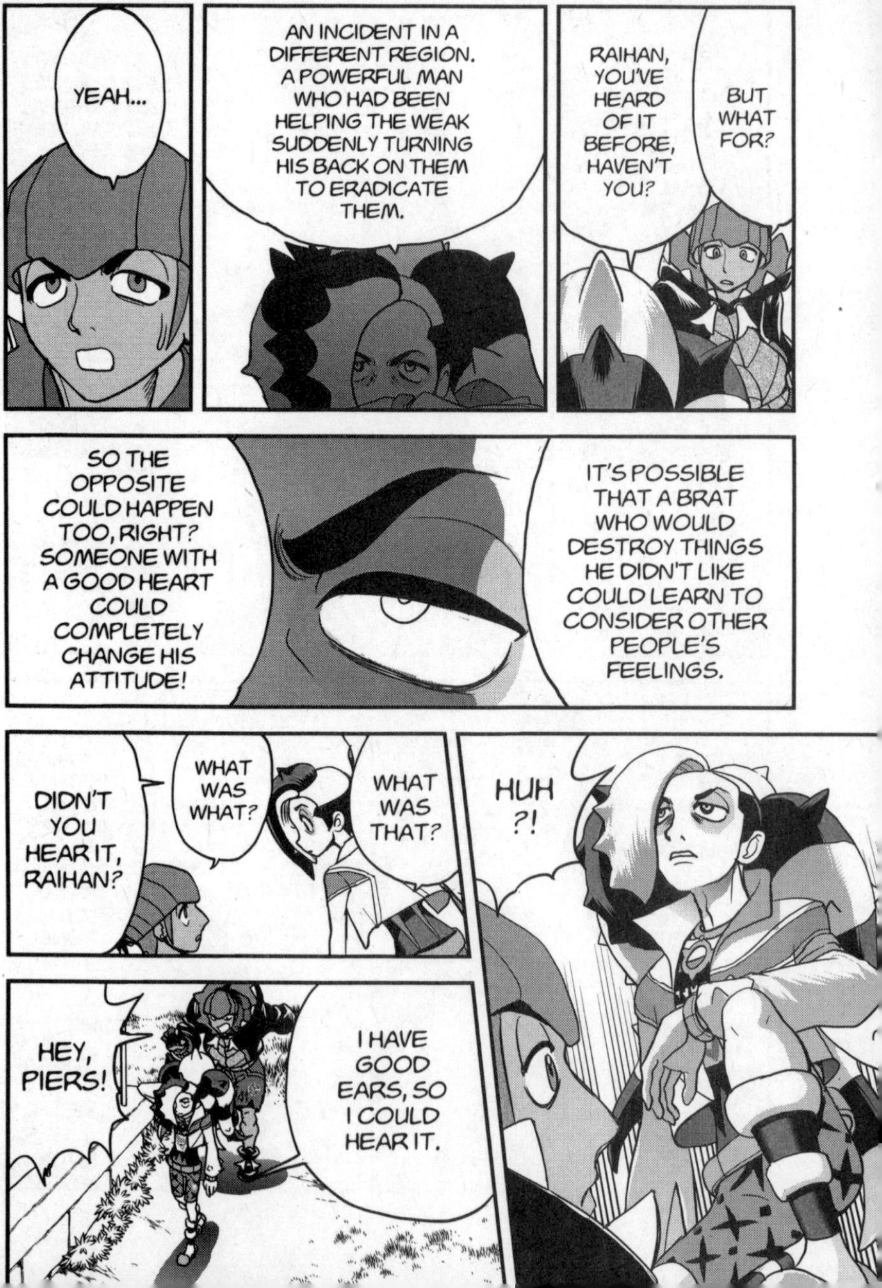
RAIHAN, YOU'VE HEARD OF IT BEFORE, HAVEN'T YOU?
BUT WHAT FOR?
AN INCIDENT IN A DIFFERENT REGION. A POWERFUL MAN WHO HAD BEEN HELPING THE WEAK SUDDENLY TURNING HIS BACK ON THEM TO ERADICATE THEM.
YEAH...
IT'S POSSIBLE THAT A BRAT WHO WOULD DESTROY THINGS HE DIDN'T LIKE COULD LEARN TO CONSIDER OTHER PEOPLE'S FEELINGS.
SO THE OPPOSITE COULD HAPPEN TOO, RIGHT? SOMEONE WITH A GOOD HEART COULD COMPLETELY CHANGE HIS ATTITUDE!
HUH ?!
WHAT WAS THAT?
WHAT WAS WHAT?
DIDN'T YOU HEAR IT, RAIHAN?
I HAVE GOOD EARS, SO I COULD HEAR IT.
HEY, PIERS!

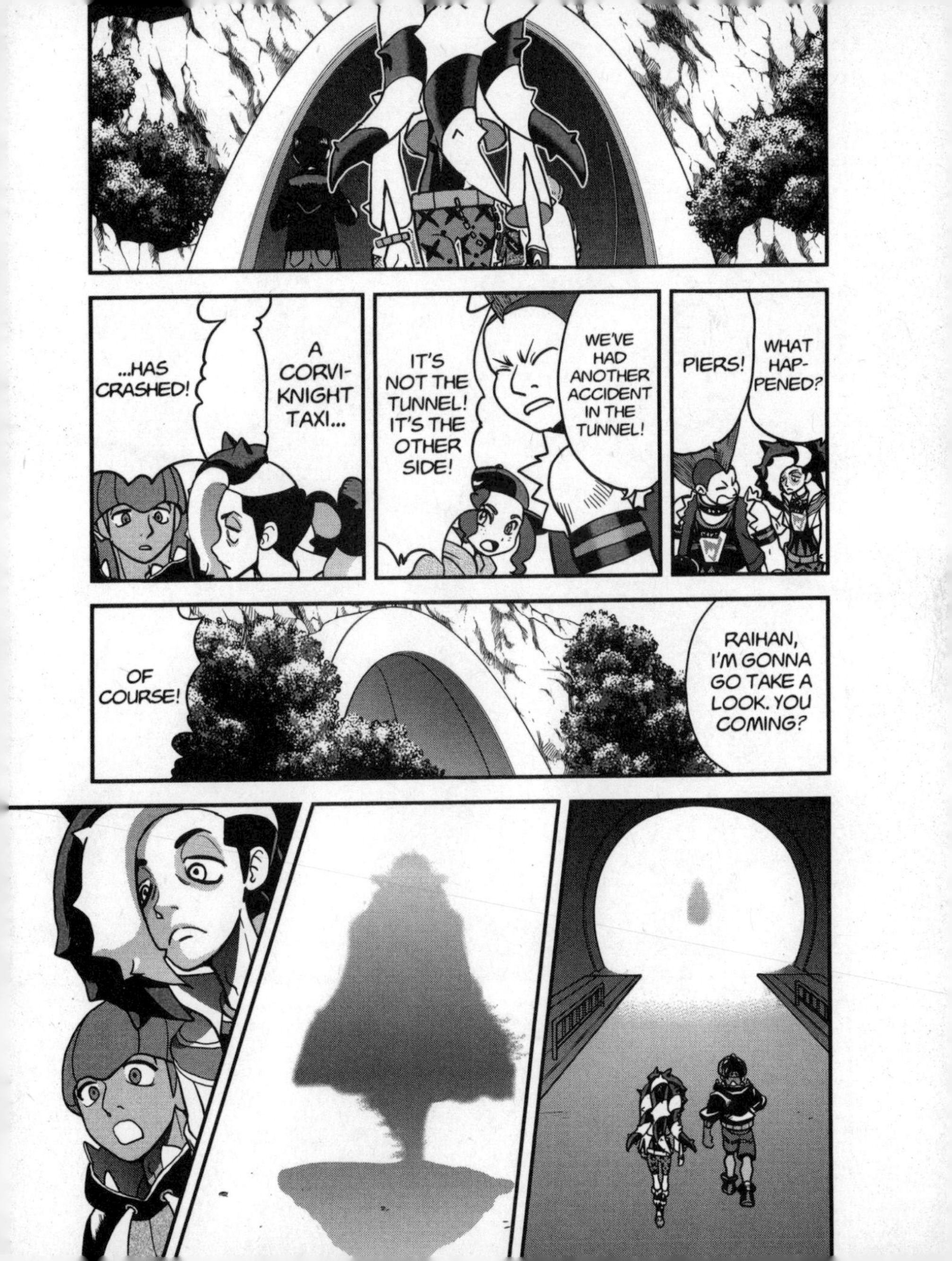
WHAT HAPPENED?
PIERS!
WE'VE HAD ANOTHER ACCIDENT IN THE TUNNEL!
IT'S NOT THE TUNNEL! IT'S THE OTHER SIDE!
A CORVIKNIGHT TAXI...
...HAS CRASHED!
RAIHAN, I'M GONNA GO TAKE A LOOK. YOU COMING?
OF COURSE!

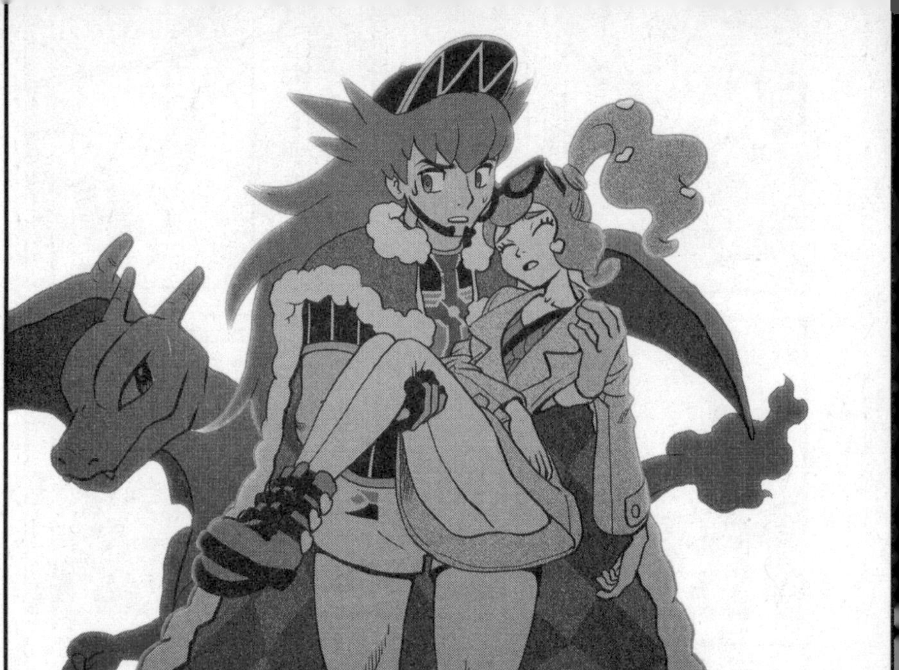

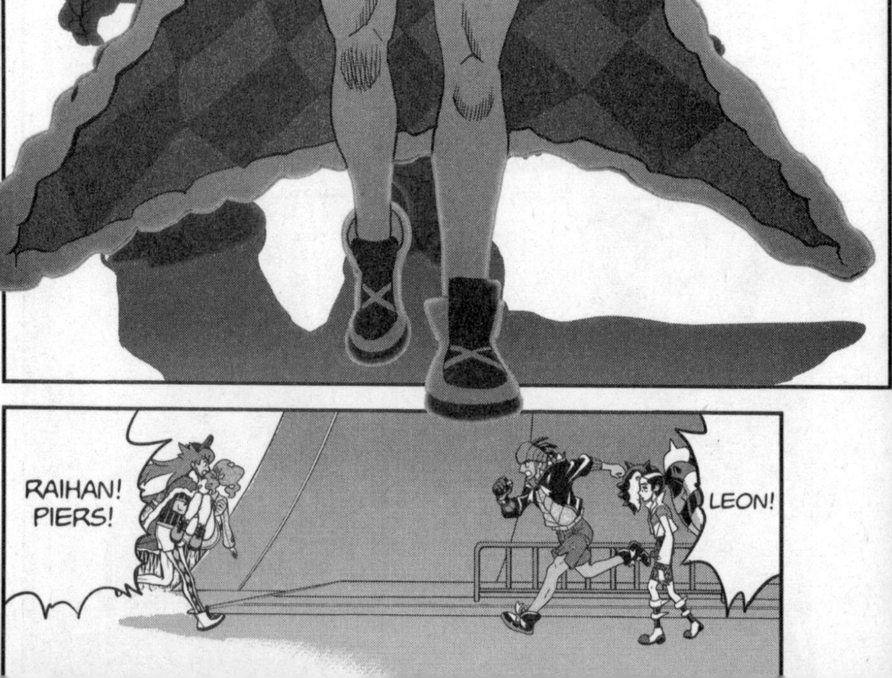
LEON!
RAIHAN!
PIERS!

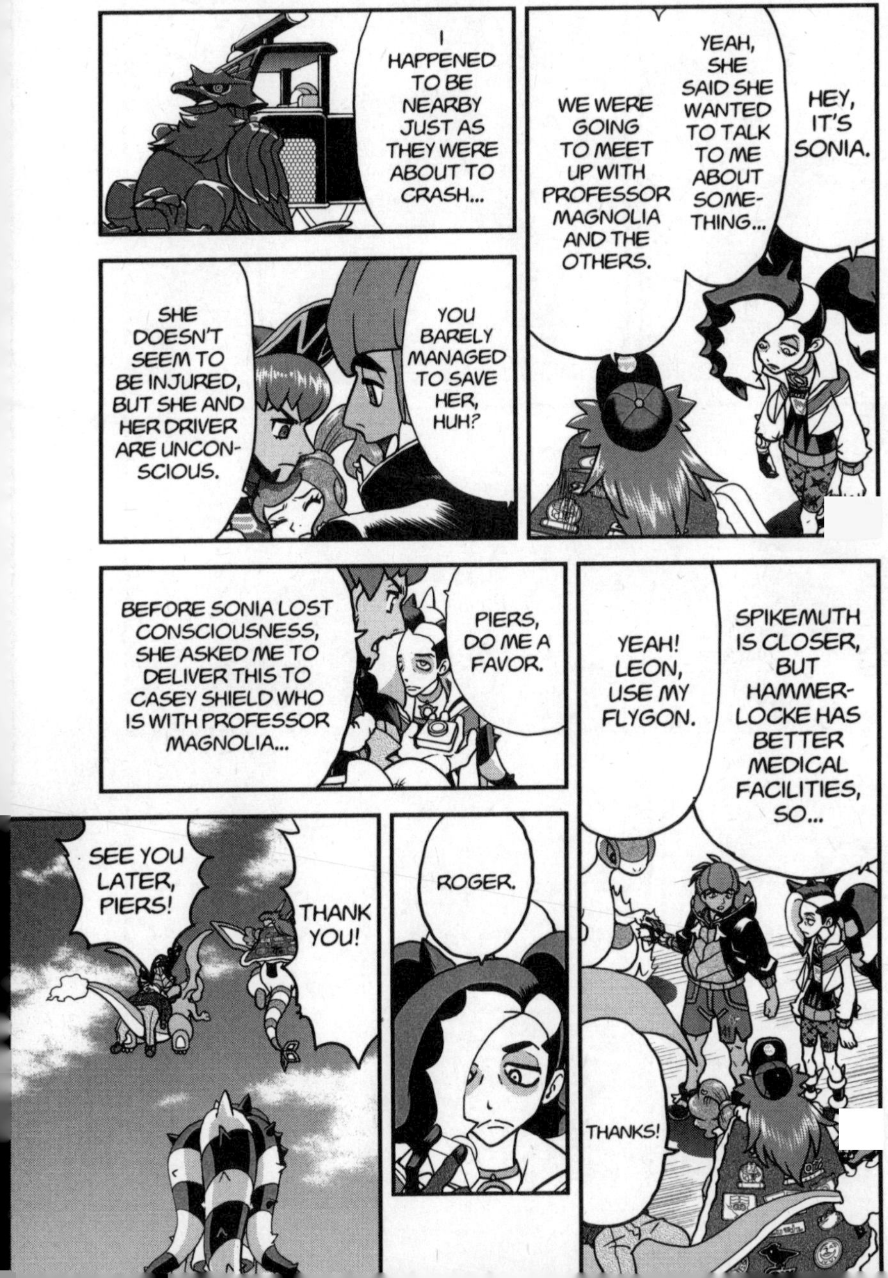
HEY, IT'S SONIA.
YEAH, SHE SAID SHE WANTED TO TALK TO ME ABOUT SOME-THING...
WE WERE GOING TO MEET UP WITH PROFESSOR MAGNOLIA AND THE OTHERS.
I HAPPENED TO BE NEARBY JUST AS THEY WERE ABOUT TO CRASH...
YOU BARELY MANAGED TO SAVE HER, HUH?
SHE DOESN'T SEEM TO BE INJURED, BUT SHE AND HER DRIVER ARE UNCON-SCIOUS.
SPIKEMUTH IS CLOSER, BUT HAMMER-LOCKE HAS BETTER MEDICAL FACILITIES, SO...
YEAH! LEON, USE MY FLYGON.
THANKS!
PIERS, DO ME A FAVOR.
BEFORE SONIA LOST CONSCIOUSNESS, SHE ASKED ME TO DELIVER THIS TO CASEY SHIELD WHO IS WITH PROFESSOR MAGNOLIA...
ROGER.
SEE YOU LATER, PIERS!
THANK YOU!

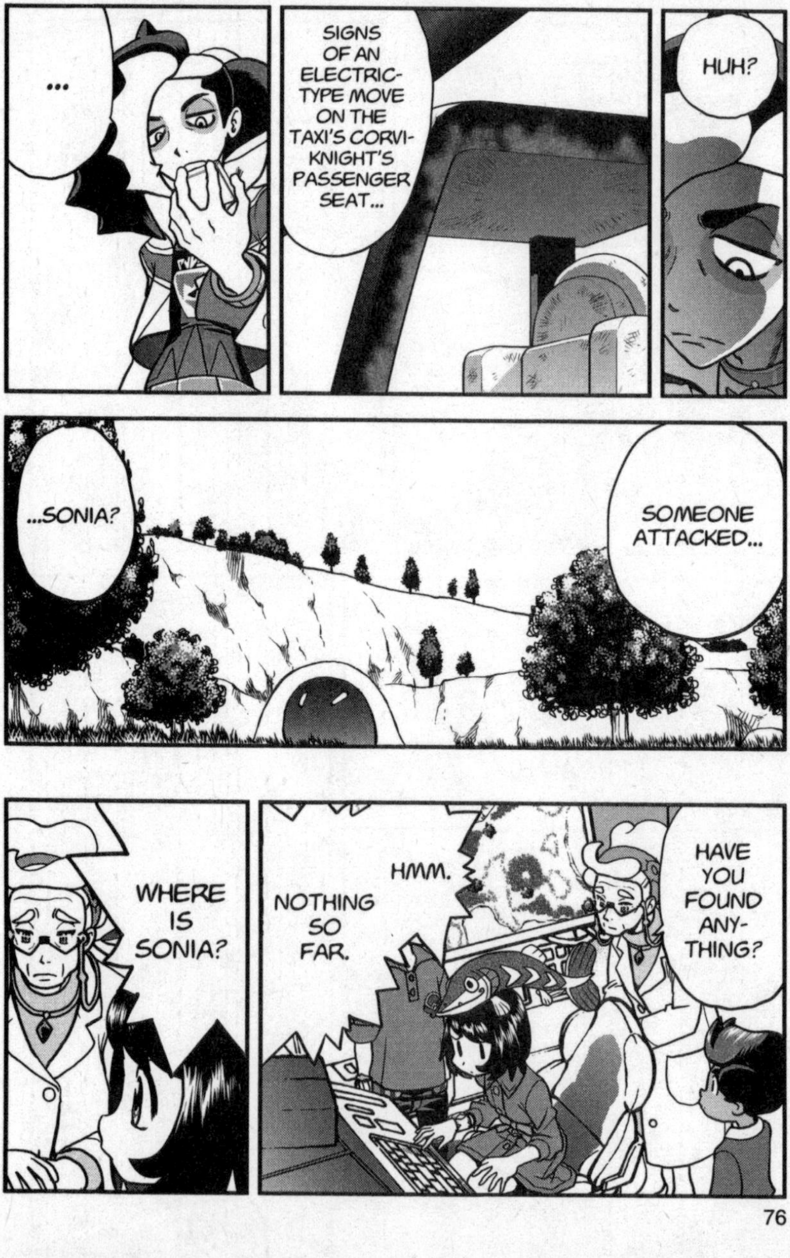
HUH?
SIGNS OF AN ELECTRIC-TYPE MOVE ON THE TAXI'S CORVI-KNIGHT'S PASSENGER SEAT...
...
SOMEONE ATTACKED...
...SONIA?
HAVE YOU FOUND ANY-THING?
HMM.
NOTHING SO FAR.
WHERE IS SONIA?

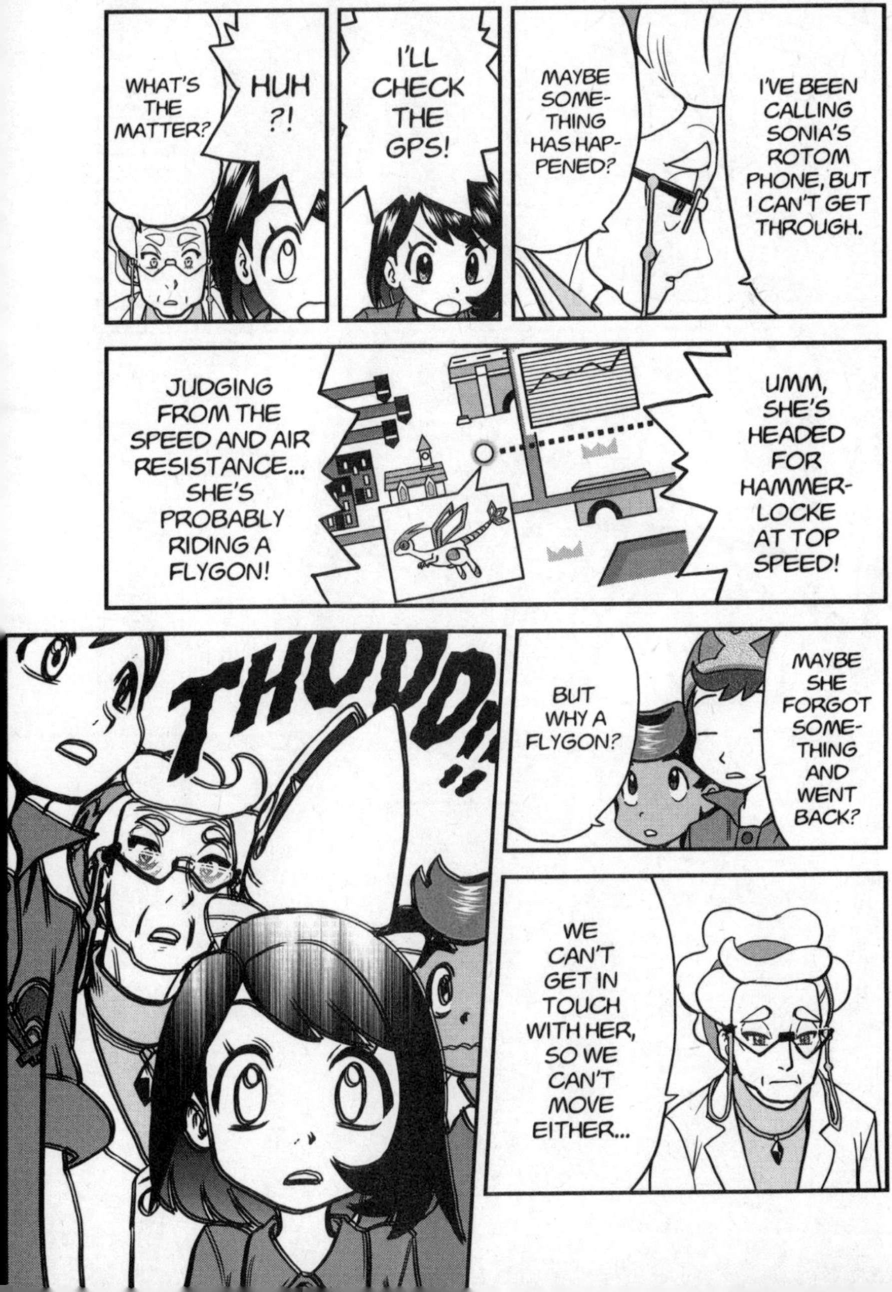
I'VE BEEN CALLING SONIA'S ROTOM PHONE, BUT I CAN'T GET THROUGH.
MAYBE SOMETHING HAS HAPPENED?
I'LL CHECK THE GPS!
HUH ?!
WHAT'S THE MATTER?
UMM, SHE'S HEADED FOR HAMMERLOCKE AT TOP SPEED!
JUDGING FROM THE SPEED AND AIR RESISTANCE... SHE'S PROBABLY RIDING A FLYGON!
MAYBE SHE FORGOT SOMETHING AND WENT BACK?
BUT WHY A FLYGON?
WE CAN'T GET IN TOUCH WITH HER, SO WE CAN'T MOVE EITHER...
THUDD!!

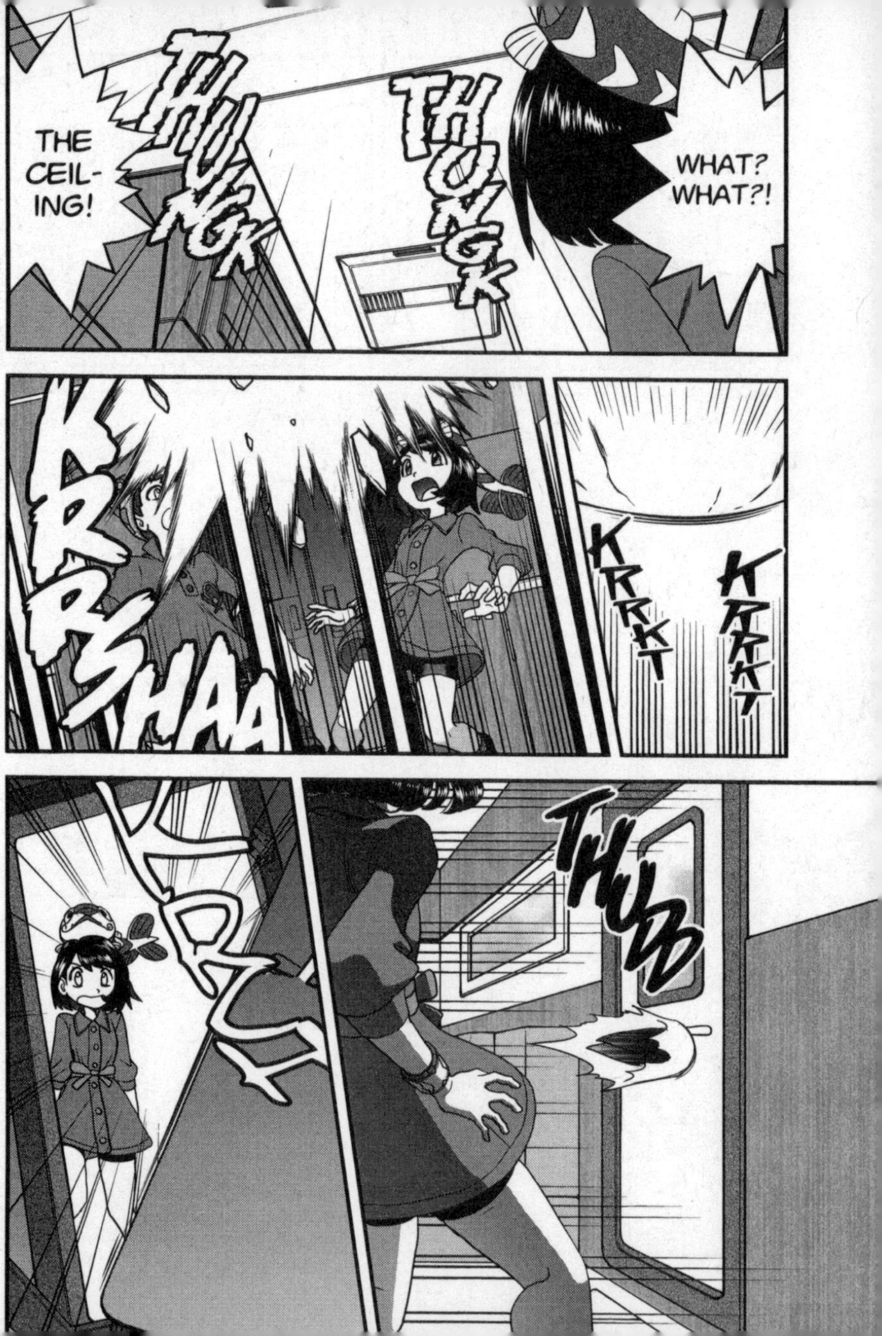
WHAT? WHAT?!
THONGK
THUNGK
THE CEIL-ING!
KRRKT KRRKT
THUDD

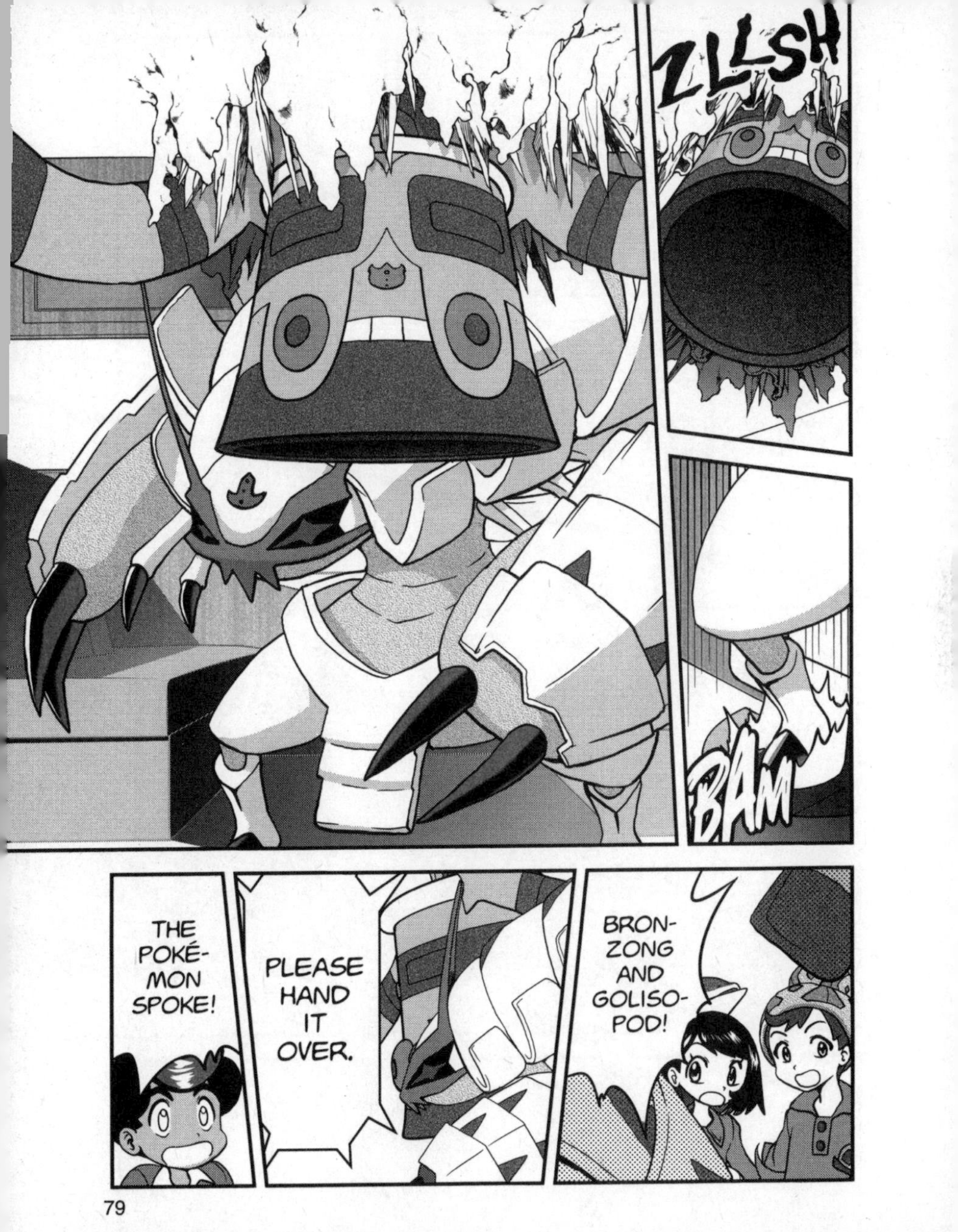
ZLLSH
BAM
BRON-ZONG AND GOLISO-POD!
PLEASE HAND IT OVER.
THE POKÉ-MON SPOKE!

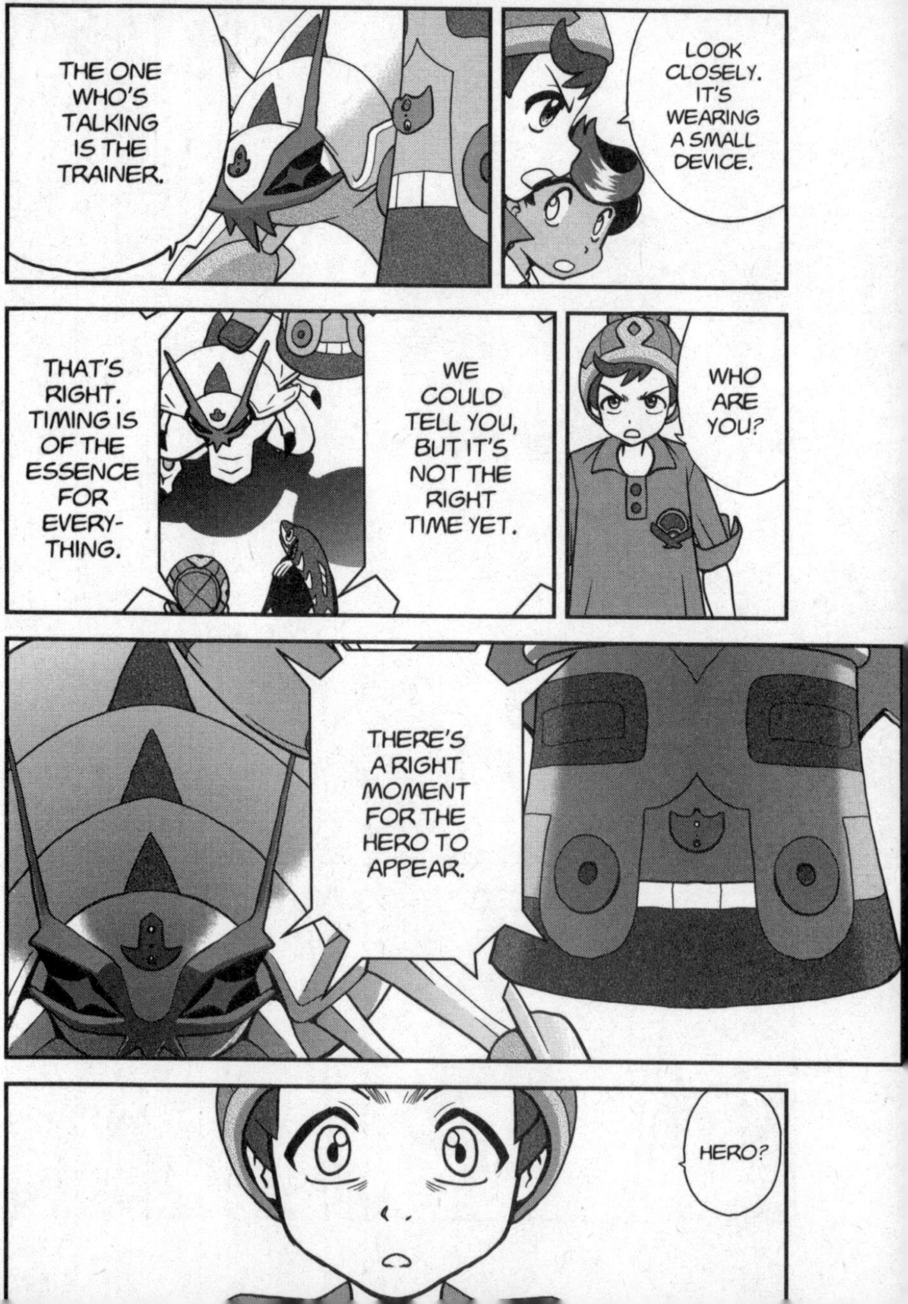
LOOK CLOSELY. IT'S WEARING A SMALL DEVICE.
THE ONE WHO'S TALKING IS THE TRAINER.
WHO ARE YOU?
WE COULD TELL YOU, BUT IT'S NOT THE RIGHT TIME YET.
THAT'S RIGHT. TIMING IS OF THE ESSENCE FOR EVERY-THING.
THERE'S A RIGHT MOMENT FOR THE HERO TO APPEAR.
HERO?

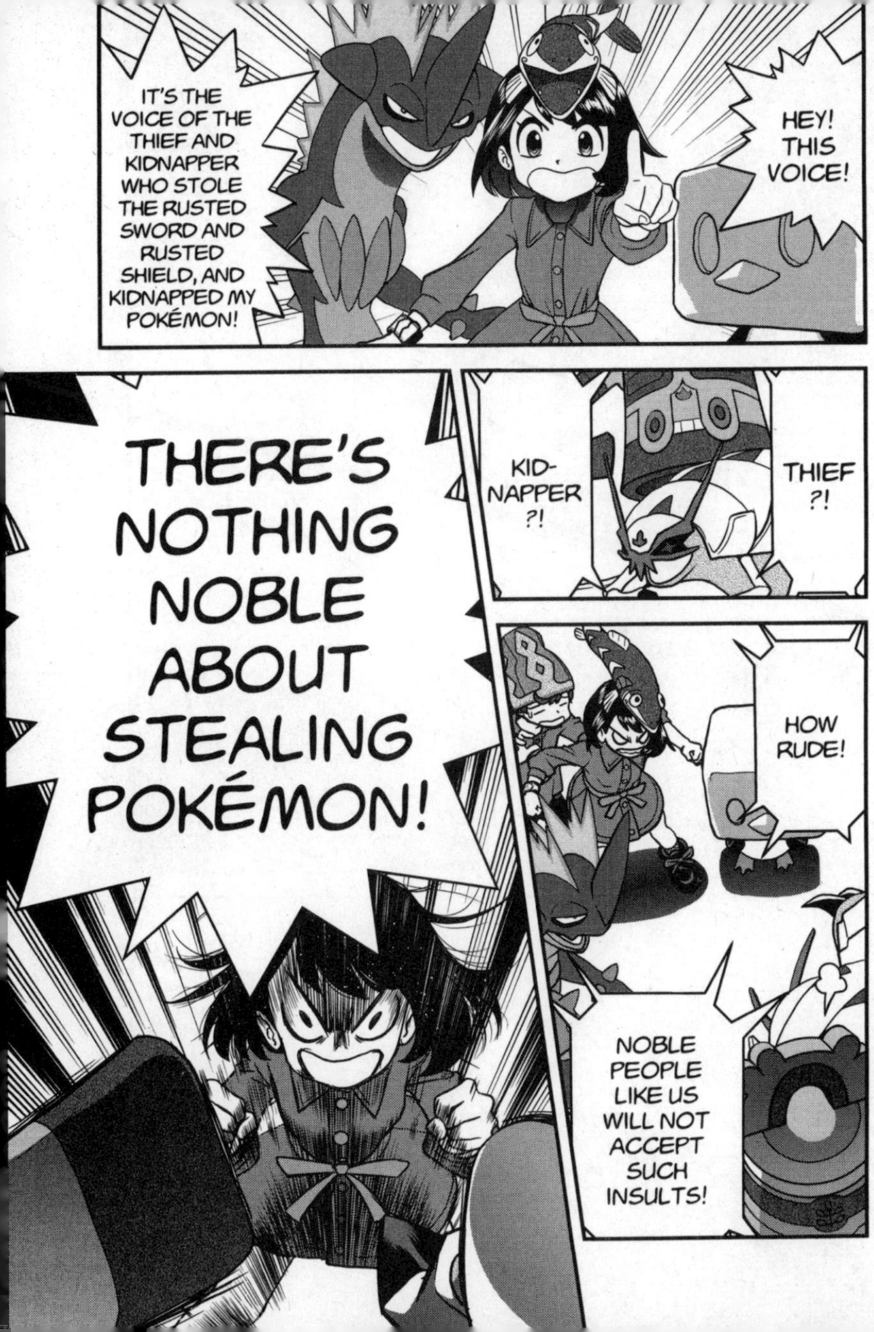
HEY! THIS VOICE!
IT'S THE VOICE OF THE THIEF AND KIDNAPPER WHO STOLE THE RUSTED SWORD AND RUSTED SHIELD, AND KIDNAPPED MY POKÉMON!
THIEF ?!
KID-NAPPER ?!
HOW RUDE!
NOBLE PEOPLE LIKE US WILL NOT ACCEPT SUCH INSULTS!
THERE'S NOTHING NOBLE ABOUT STEALING POKÉMON!

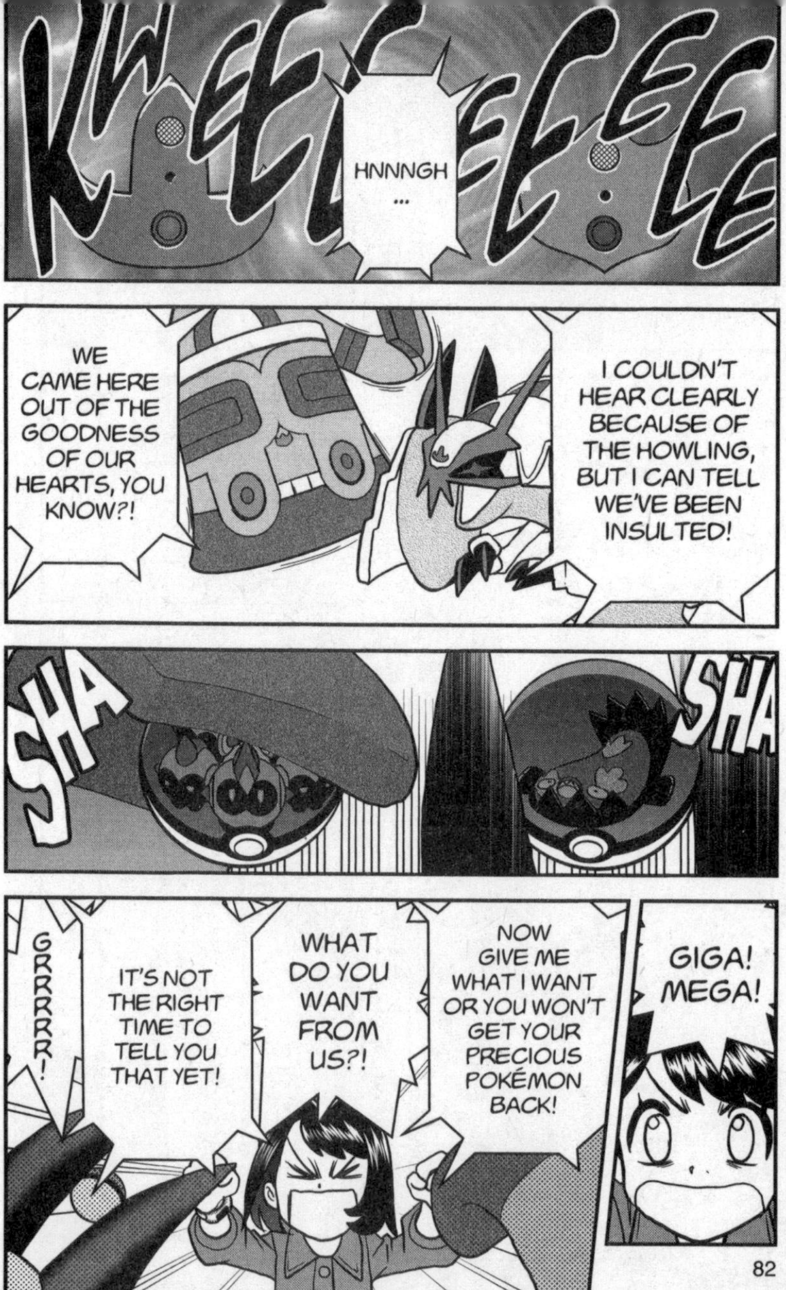
KWEEEEEEEEEE
HNNNGH ...
I COULDN'T HEAR CLEARLY BECAUSE OF THE HOWLING, BUT I CAN TELL WE'VE BEEN INSULTED!
WE CAME HERE OUT OF THE GOODNESS OF OUR HEARTS, YOU KNOW?!
SHA
SHA
GIGA! MEGA!
NOW GIVE ME WHAT I WANT OR YOU WON'T GET YOUR PRECIOUS POKÉMON BACK!
WHAT DO YOU WANT FROM US?!
IT'S NOT THE RIGHT TIME TO TELL YOU THAT YET!
GRRRRR!

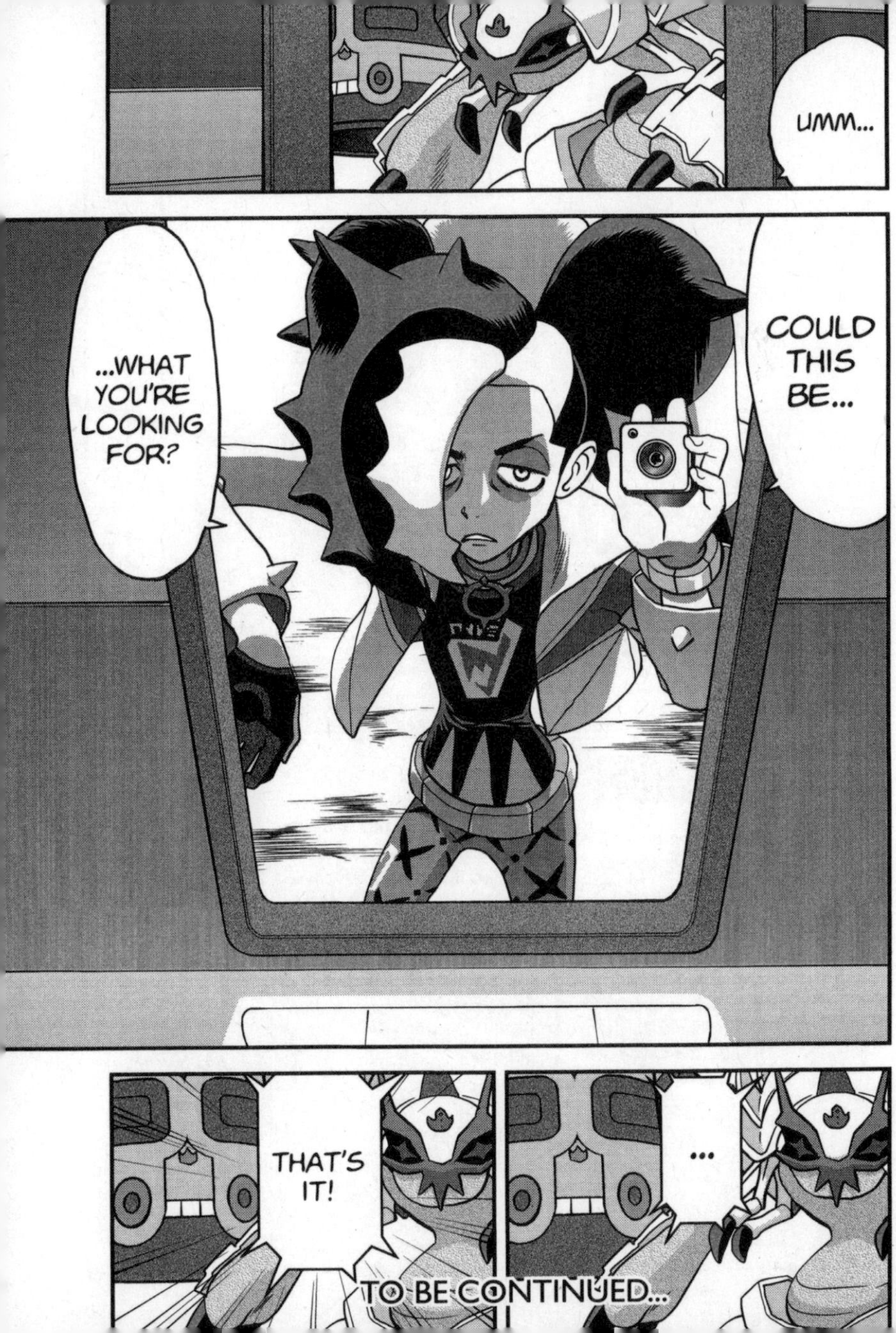
UMM...
COULD THIS BE...
...WHAT YOU'RE LOOKING FOR?
...
THAT'S IT!
TO BE CONTINUED...

GIGANTAMAX GARBODOR

HEIGHT	68'11"+
WEIGHT	??? lbs

ORDINARY

GARBODOR

HEIGHT	6'03"
WEIGHT	236.6 lbs

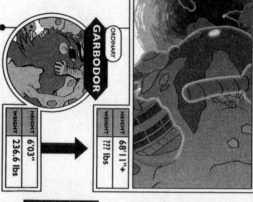

TYPE:	Poison
ABILITY:	Stench Weak Armor
G-MAX MOVE:	G-Max Malodor

An interesting Pokémon whose toxic gas has become much thicker. The gas congeals into masses shaped like discarded toys. Gigantamax Garbodor looks more ominous than its usual form. If the toxic gas from its mouth and fingers engulfs you, the toxins will seep in all the way down to your bones.

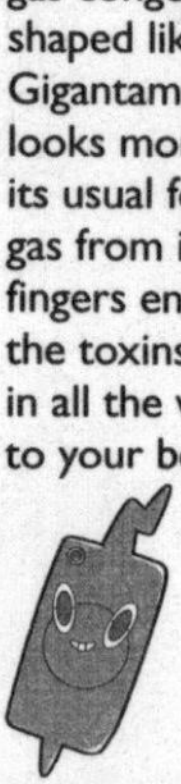

STRATEGY NOTES

The Poison-type move used by Gigantamax Garbodor is G-Max Malodor. Its poison causes extreme agony. On top of that, its ability, Stench, has a chance of making its opponent flinch, making the battle even more dangerous.

Hidenori Kusaka is the writer for *Pokémon Adventures*. Running continuously for over 25 years, *Pokémon Adventures* is the only manga series to completely cover all the *Pokémon* games and has become one of the most popular series of all time. In addition to writing manga, he also edits children's books and plans mixed-media projects for Shogakukan's children's magazines. He uses the Pokémon Electrode as his author portrait.

Satoshi Yamamoto is the artist for *Pokémon Adventures*, which he began working on in 2001, starting with volume 10. Yamamoto launched his manga career in 1993 with the horror-action title *Kimen Senshi*, which ran in Shogakukan's *Weekly Shonen Sunday* magazine, followed by the series *Kaze no Denshosha*. Yamamoto's favorite manga creators/artists include FUJIKO F FUJIO (*Doraemon*), Yukinobu Hoshino (*2001 Nights*), and Katsuhiro Otomo (*Akira*). He loves films, monsters, detective novels, and punk rock music. He uses the Pokémon Swalot as his artist portrait.

Pokémon: Sword & Shield
Volume 7
VIZ Media Edition

Story by HIDENORI KUSAKA
Art by SATOSHI YAMAMOTO

©2023 Pokémon.
©1995–2022 Nintendo / Creatures Inc. / GAME FREAK inc.
TM, ®, and character names are trademarks of Nintendo.
© 2020 Hidenori KUSAKA, Satoshi YAMAMOTO
All rights reserved.
Original Japanese edition published by SHOGAKUKAN.
English translation rights in the United States of America, Canada, the United Kingdom,
Ireland, Australia and New Zealand arranged with SHOGAKUKAN.

Original Cover Design—Hiroyuki KAWASOME (grafio)

Translation—Tetsuichiro Miyaki
English Adaptation—Molly Tanzer
Touch-Up & Lettering—Annaliese "Ace" Christman
Design—Alice Lewis
Editor—Joel Enos

Special thanks to Trish Ledoux at at The Pokémon Company International.

The stories, characters, and incidents mentioned
in this publication are entirely fictional.

No portion of this book may be reproduced or transmitted
in any form or by any means without written permission
from the copyright holders.

Printed in the U.S.A.

Published by VIZ Media, LLC
P.O. Box 77010
San Francisco, CA 94107

10 9 8 7 6 5 4 3 2 1
First printing, August 2023

PARENTAL ADVISORY
POKÉMON: SWORD & SHIELD is rated A
and is suitable for readers of all ages.

viz.com

Coming Next Volume

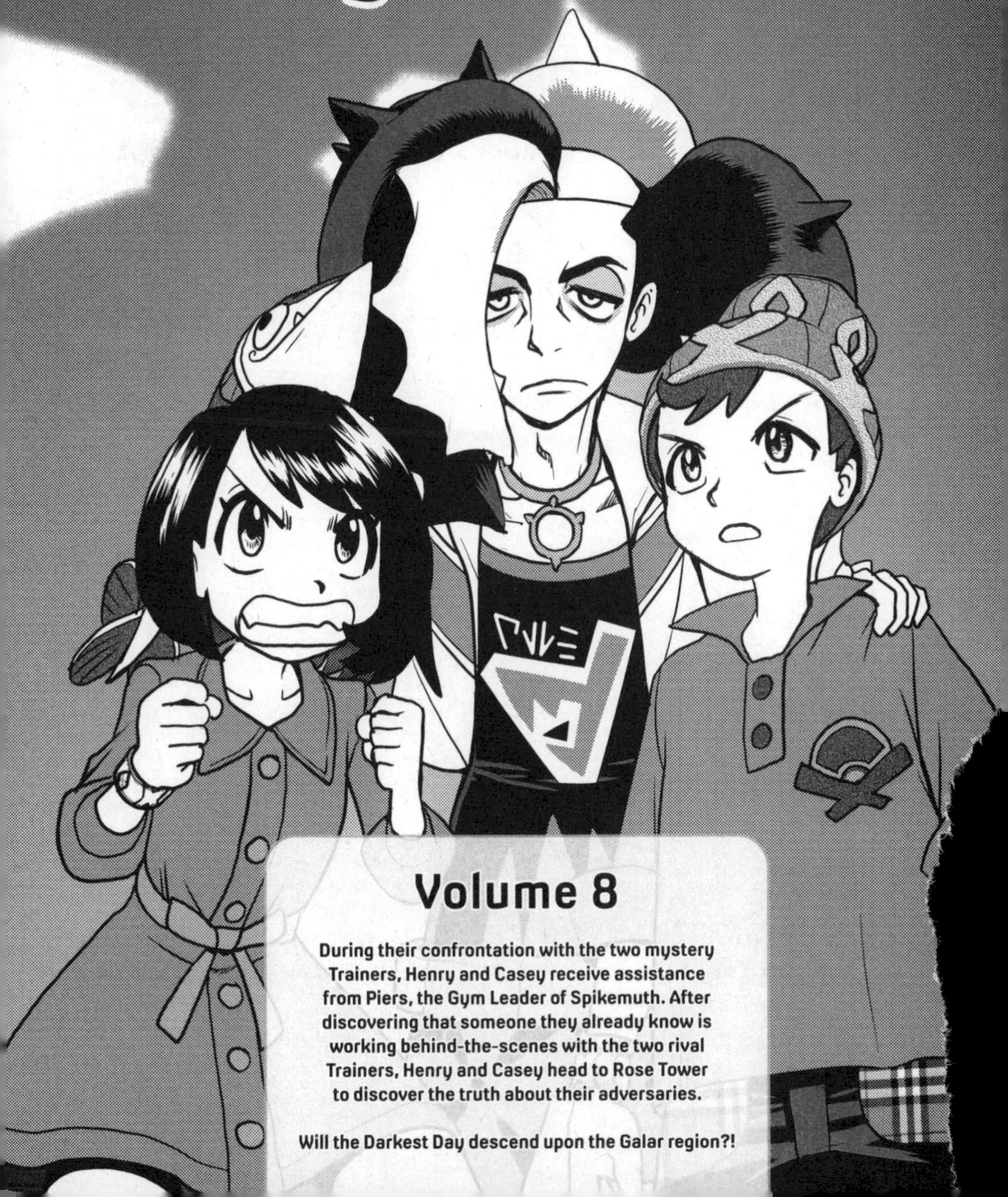

Volume 8

During their confrontation with the two mystery Trainers, Henry and Casey receive assistance from Piers, the Gym Leader of Spikemuth. After discovering that someone they already know is working behind-the-scenes with the two rival Trainers, Henry and Casey head to Rose Tower to discover the truth about their adversaries.

Will the Darkest Day descend upon the Galar region?!

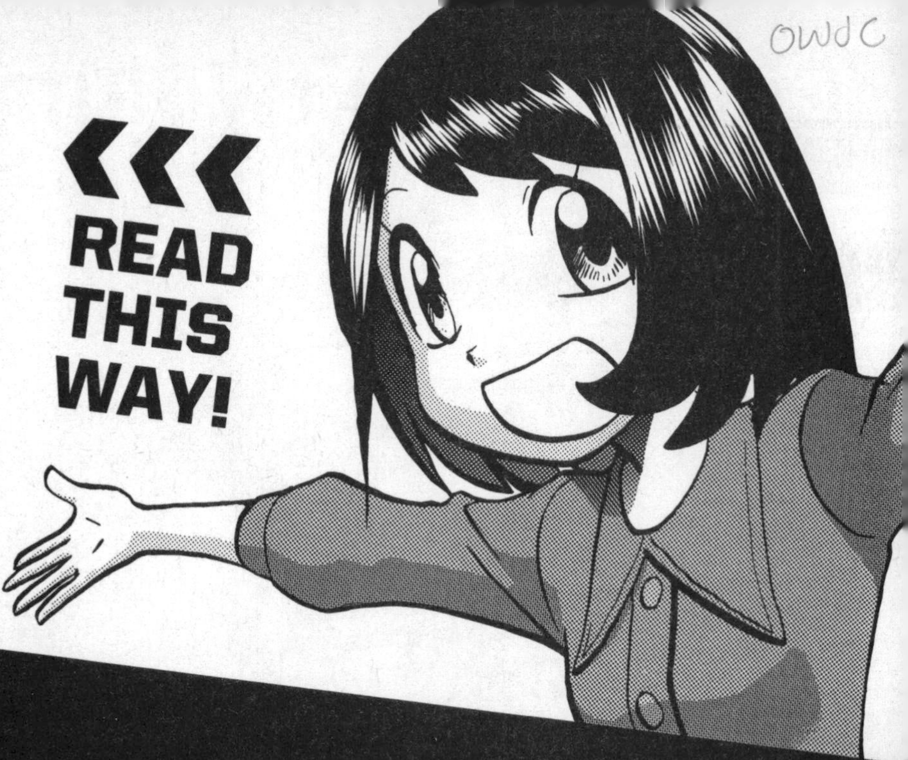
READ THIS WAY!

THIS IS THE END OF THIS GRAPHIC NOVEL!

To properly enjoy this VIZ Media graphic novel, please turn it around and begin reading from right to left.

This book has been printed in the original Japanese format in order to preserve the orientation of the original artwork. Have fun with it!

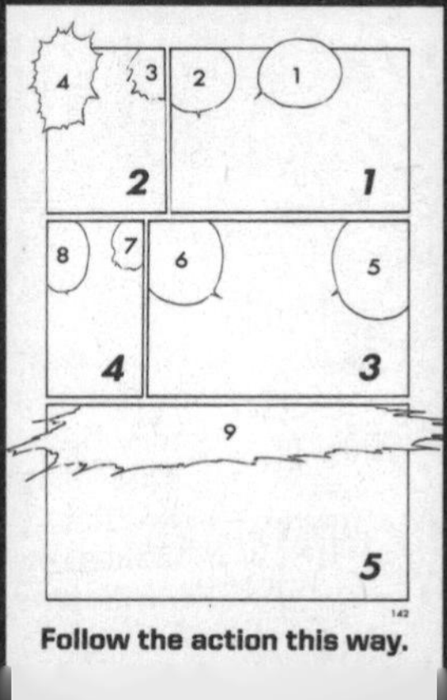

Follow the action this way.